The City Below the Cloud

A Novella

Written by
T. S. Galindo

Edited by
S. B. Galindo

ISBN: 9781693367533

For
Sam

Chapter One | The Tooth

Where are my dreams?

Kalan opened her eyes into complete darkness. Her usually vivid dreams were absent; a barren sleep, like she'd been drifting in a void for hours. The quiet blackness when her eyes were closed, and the quiet blackness when her eyes were open, felt no different to her. She rolled onto her side. When her jaw touched the mattress a spike of pain tunneled its way through one of her molars.

She sat up and groped the floor in the darkness for the glowbe, a sphere that acted as an area light. She found it and touched the metal contacts. Soft white light splattered the bare concrete walls. Sett groaned from the other side of the mattress and curled up tighter, covering her face with her arm.

Kalan probed her mouth with her fingers. It felt like a hot needle was stabbing through one of her teeth. She held her breath and squinted through the pain as she grabbed the offending tooth, wiggled it loose, and extracted it easily. The pain vanished. She examined it in the glowbe light.

It looks fine, no rot or anything; but there's no blood.

She worked her tongue into the new gap and flexed her jaw, biting down a few times.

No blood there either; and the pain's gone. If there's no pain, it's fine, I guess. I'll try to remember to check on it later. I don't want to waste charge on a mender unless I have to.

Kalan pulled a loose thread from the mattress and hung the tooth around her neck next to her coin with a '0' on it. When she finished, she touched off the glowbe and turned to lay back down. The moment her head touched the mattress, a strobing light and screeching alarm blared through the room.

Both Sett and Kalan jolted awake. Kalan frantically crawled through the moments of darkness and light trying to find the source while Sett pressed her hands to her ears and screamed to block out the noise. Kalan found the task coordinator, the source, and turned it off. The darkness returned. Sett stopped screaming a second later. Their ears throbbed in the silence.

"What was that? Why'd you set an alert?" Sett complained.

"I didn't. I never do," Kalan said as she illuminated the glowbe and stuck it to the wall. She started working the control rings on the task coordinator, a small cylindrical device with a lighted display. It acted as a mobile job board by connecting to the city's computers.

"No, wait. There IS a task saved, but I didn't save it, I swear. Look, it's on the 575th floor. That doesn't even make sense. No building goes that high. This thing must be busted," she said.

Sett huffed, rolled back onto the mattress, and said, "well get a new one, and do it quick. This isn't how I wanna wake up."

Kalan got up and started putting on her coverall while saying, "since when are you in charge, little sis?"

Sett made a disgruntled noise and covered her eyes with her arm again. Kalan chuckled and continued getting ready. She buckled a harness covered in lights over her torso, hung her face mask around her neck, grabbed her stun-baton, and picked up the defective task coordinator. She grabbed the glowbe and took it with her to the door of the unit. The moving light source highlighted the smallness of the room, just enough for a mattress and a small human waste reclamator in the back corner. She slid open the door and checked the timer.

"Two hours left on the unit. Sleep fast. If you think a broken task coordinator is a nasty way to wake up, try getting washed out again," Kalan said.

They'd been washed out of two units before because of oversleeping. It was a harrowing experience. Units were rented by the minute with a maximum of twelve hours. When the timer ran out, the door automatically opened, leaving the occupants exposed; ten seconds later, if the unit was not evacuated, or the timer paid, alarms would come on, ten seconds after that the unit would be flooded with acid-rain water; they called this getting washed out.

Kalan delluminated the glowbe and tossed it onto the mattress next to Sett. Sett grunted again and waved her arm in the air at Kalan.

"I'll meet you at the yards later," Kalan said as she stepped into the hallway and slid the door closed. She trekked through the maze of narrow hallways lit with pale, neon green light strips. She had to step over the huddled bodies of exhausted people who hadn't been able to find an open unit. It was better than sleeping outside, but they risked having their belongings stolen.

She passed the bay of elevators; they cost ten joules per level; an unnecessary luxury on the third floor of a building. She took the stairs to the ground floor.

The stairwell was lit blue by a light rope hung from the top of the building through the center of the coiled steps. To save energy, the rope illuminated from top to bottom every few seconds in a cascading pattern. The effect was like light dripping from the top of the seemingly endless helical shaft.

The echoing of a hundred floors of doors opening and closing and the pattering feet of people using the stairs always made her feel somehow connected to the city and its inhabitants. She sat down on the final step and pulled out the task coordinator.

Let's see if it at least works enough to find a job, she thought while she twisted the control rings looking through the available tasks. *Too far. Too far. Too big a job. Doesn't pay enough. Here we go, this'll do. I should be able to get there in time.*

She hung the device on her harness so she could see the flat end of it easily. It displayed an arrow pointing toward the task she'd chosen and the distance to it. She got up and made her way out to the street.

The familiar acrid scent and accompanying fog from a light acid-rain swirled around her as she slid the door open. She strapped on her filter mask and put up her hood. The long term effects of the near-constant acid rains had reduced life spans to 40 years if filter masks were worn regularly; much less if not. The sound of the rain mingled with the hundreds of people shuffling in all directions. They collided and pressed their way through the living obstacles between them and their goals.

She moved into the crowd. The sound of the street was a cacophonous echo of millions of footfalls, puddles splashing, raindrops on vinyl and concrete, and the wind groaning through the mile-high monolithic buildings. She checked the arrow on her task coordinator and tried to push herself in that general direction. The process was more about resisting being shoved in the directions she didn't want to go rather than actively propelling herself toward where she did want to go.

The sky was a permanent black Cloud of smog that choked the city and its inhabitants. Her view was cropped on all sides by the windowless, concrete buildings; most stopped short of the Cloud, but some ascended into its depths to unknown heights. They were vertical fields of acid-scarred concrete stretching upward. Metal walkways connected them, crisscrossing the sky in seemingly random arrangements. They helped to mitigate the traffic of bodies by layering the travelers on top of each other. The streets were lit by hundreds of neon signs littering the sides of the buildings, moving around slowly on wall-gripping treads. Otherwise, people had to provide their own light to navigate in the claustrophobically smogged city.

The Cloud covered the entire metropolis, permanently blotting out the sun. The inhabitants of the city knew nothing of the sun, or of day or night. The climate and temperature remained relatively consistent all year; further isolating the city dwellers from natural temporal machinations. They had no basis for measuring time beyond the twelve-hour cycles and no way to plan ahead out of a constant need to secure their immediate basic needs. They lived in moments and memories of events rather than milestones or ages. Time moved for them not at all and all at once.

The section of the city that Sett and Kalan primarily stayed in was known as the mushroom district. The walls of the buildings were covered in blankets of lichen and crops of other fungi. Many mushroom species dotted the lichen. Large shelf mushrooms provided some respite from the rain, like awnings; bioluminescent caps added extra light in the suffocating darkness. When it rained, the vertical mushroom forests bloomed; caps blossomed and stalks stretched to their maximum to catch the falling water like a great, many-tentacled beast reaching into the inky Cloud. The chemicals, toxic to humans, were nourishing to these once-exotic species. It was a symbiotic relationship with the buildings; the concrete structures provided support and surface area for the fungi, and the fungi protected the buildings from the acid by consuming it before it came in contact and corroded the concrete. Outside the mushroom district, the buildings required a coating of chemical solvents to protect them.

The mushrooms grew somewhat uncontained, however, and had to be culled from bridges and doorways and vents. This was Kalan's job, she was a scrubber. She ascended the towers to scrub off lichen and mushrooms growing in inconvenient places.

She continued to shove her way through the crowd toward her first job of the cycle.

Chapter Two | The Task

The rain had subsided by the time Kalan reached the task terminal. The number of people had thinned to a manageable swarm, but it still took her much longer than usual to get there. Crowd densities followed patterns. Those not bound by timing schedules had learned to avoid them. She cursed the broken task coordinator for waking her up when it did, throwing off her timing.

The city spread across the ground like an infection from a mine at the base of a mountain. The mine was a gaping wound in the earth where people extracted minerals and other precious materials. The city mostly consisted of refineries and processing plants. Everything not directly linked to the mine was in service of keeping it running. There were just enough available resources to house and feed the people to keep a working population, lest production fall short.

Work shifts in the mine switched at the cycle changes, meaning there were large groups of people getting on the large elevators to go down, and worn-out people returning from a full cycle of work. Thus, the crowds were most extreme just before and after the start of a cycle. Kalan's work wasn't based on schedules, so she could choose her own hours, though she still had to compete with the other scrubbers for available tasks.

Any tasks, including working in the mines or refineries, paid just enough to get someone through a cycle or less. It was impossible to store up any significant amount of charge, the currency of the city. When groups of people tried to pool their resources, there still wasn't enough to make a difference. Groups were just as economically vulnerable, sometimes more so, than individuals, causing people to become isolated. For most inhabitants of the city, the norm was isolation and paranoia.

Kalan placed her defective task coordinator in the terminal, claiming the job for herself. A compartment opened on the side of the machine containing the necessary tools; a mobile platform, a scrub-brush, and a pair of glasses fitted with augmented-reality displays. She collected the items and put the glasses on, which showed her where the job site was.

Good, it's just across the street.

The terminals weren't always close to the task; she often had to haul the heavy platform several blocks.

She navigated through the dwindling crowd and set up the platform. The tiny tendrils on the omnidirectional treads reached out and gripped the concrete wall as if alive. Once attached, it straightened itself out and performed a dance-like calibration routine. She sat down and gripped the sides as it jolted upward and began ascending the building. Occasionally, the treads would slip on the lichen and rarely, they'd lose grip entirely. This had never happened to her, but she'd seen the wreckages and known people who'd been unlucky.

Despite the looming possibility of death, this was Kalan's favorite part of being a scrubber. She loved watching the city descend below her, and she loved the rare opportunity to be alone in a city so densely populated. The ever-present feeling of threat fell away the further she got from the river of strangers. The sounds of the streets reverberated distantly around her with a haunting, unreal quality. Not being part of the constant motion of the crowds gave her a dysphoric sense of stillness despite the fact that she was literally moving with the platform. Up there, she was alone and important. Her world was at once the vast open-air between the buildings, stretching as far as the Cloud allowed her to see, and the limited domain of the tiny platform.

She watched the people below. Most wore large, ill-fitting raincoats pieced together from scraps of vinyl on top of worn, mismatched garments or draped fabric. Everyone had bald or shaved heads to reduce the risk of lice. Many were covered in dirt and mud from the mines or colored mineral residue from the refineries. Most had prosthetics of some kind; typically, a hand or arm; eyes were also common.

Legs were harder to come by. If someone needed a leg prosthetic, they rarely lasted long enough to find a replacement.

Skin color had become a spectrum between charcoal-black and chalk-white. The lack of sunlight and the heavy environmental impact of the mined minerals and refinery exhaust had changed how people's skin pigments expressed themselves. The extremes of the color range were pretty rare; most skin was within a small range of greys. This allowed other attributes to be a larger distinguishing factor, such as how rough or smooth, how moist or dry, or how varied or consistent the gradients were. The change took many generations, but it eliminated most skin-color based prejudices in the city below the Cloud.

As she was carried further upward she started to lose sight of individuals; only the lights were visible now. To supplement the light from the neon signs, people carried small handheld lights and threaded glow-wire into their clothes. From above, it was a swirling river of light flowing through the black voids of the buildings with the signs on the walls drifting like neon phantoms haunting the streets.

The platform stopped at an air vent on the building. Normally, the vent was a large round tube jutting from the concrete; it had been covered over with a net of branching, tube-like lichen thick enough to prevent airflow. She began to gather her materials when she heard a commotion from the street below.

The doors of the building across from her burst open and someone was thrown into the stream of passersby, knocking several over. Bright light flooded the street through the doorway. Kalan ducked low on the platform, clinging to the edges, while she watched the person pull something from inside their jacket.

A gun? What an idiot! Everyone knows you never touch a gun. The enforcer robots are gonna get you for sure. Here they come.

Three, two-and-a-half-meter-tall [8.2 ft] figures walked out of the building. The two on the sides emitted blinding light, flooding the entire street. The robots were slim torsos with broad shoulders and thumb-width rods for arms and legs that ended in points. They had no heads and seamless chrome bodies. They walked toward the panicking person in the street with unnaturally slow, smooth, and deliberate movements. The person pointed the gun at the robots and shot repeatedly while screaming in terror, their face was covered in tears and their voice came out in sobbing stops and starts. Kalan flinched at the dull, echoing explosions.

What are you doing? Run!

The two bullets that hit the center robot bounced off, leaving no marks or evidence of an attack. The robot didn't respond, it just kept slowly lumbering toward them. Kalan watched the scene through the wires of the grated platform. Her body shook and cold sweat beaded over her skin.

It's too late. Where'd you even find a gun? You should have just run.

She held her breath as the robot approached the shooter in the street. They hadn't tried to stand or flee. The two outer robots moved to either side of them. The light only shone from the front of their bodies, creating a surreal image from Kalan's vantage point; two cones of light blasting toward each other with the crisp shadow of the opposite robot smeared across the street in either direction. The shooter sat huddled in the fetal position drenched in shadowless light, weeping. The center robot stood ominously still over them, balanced on the points of its disproportionately thin legs.

Kalan's entire body was shaking with fear, she didn't dare breathe. As she watched the terrifying scene below, she saw a tall figure with a hooded opaque jacket standing at the corner of the building staring up at her. She couldn't see their face, but they were clearly more interested in her than the robots.

The center robot reached one of its long arms toward the shooter's head. The tip of its arm rapidly grew longer, piercing their skull, and then retracting back. The huddled figure unfolded backward and flopped onto the street, motionless. The robot retrieved the pistol from the body while the light from the two side robots vanished, creating a vacuum of darkness. Then, all three robots walked in perfect unison down the street, turned the corner, and disappeared.

Kalan continued to peer through the mesh of the platform while she waited for the adrenaline to fizzle out of her system. She watched as the people below began to go about their lives as if nothing had happened. The flow of bodies enveloped the street again.

Where'd the body go? I didn't see any glow-punks, they're usually the ones to dispose of bodies. And where'd the creep who was watching me go? Maybe down that alley? Maybe they were thinking of waiting for me to finish the job and rob my charge when I claimed it. I'll watch my back when I'm done.

Most often, people didn't have enough on them to make trying to rob them worthwhile. As soon as someone got any amount of charge, it was almost immediately spent on food or a unit. Typically, all someone owned was on their person, mostly consisting of enough clothes to keep them dry and warm. If someone knew someone was about to get some charge, they might be willing to try to steal it, however. Everyone in the city also carried a stun-baton; it was their primary, and often only, protection.

The real danger was desperation. One failed attempt to gain enough charge to afford shelter or the barely nourishing food started a quick decline into exhaustion and starvation. Deprived of food or sleep, a person's drive to survive pushed aside their rationality and everyone became a target, despite having nothing to steal. The stun-batons made short work of those imminently needy people in favor of the momentarily more fortunate.

Kalan eventually calmed down enough to start working. She strapped the mask on over the AR glasses; she had removed it when the rain slowed. Most masks were little more than filter cloth stretched over the mouth, but Kalan's was special equipment for scrubbers. It covered her whole face with a large clear plastic shield and had a second smaller mask inside, which molded around her nose and mouth. A large cylindrical filter housing attached to the front. She changed the filters often to make sure she didn't inhale anything unwanted, even beyond the acid rain. When someone got too close to certain mushrooms, they would release a large cloud of spores as a kind of defense. Most people never got close enough for this to be a hazard, but for scrubbers, it was a constant threat. Direct exposure to a cloud of spores would suffocate someone, once inhaled, there was no way to extract them in time. Even minor contaminations of spores could be fatal. They could grow inside a victim's lungs or skin, eating them slowly from the inside out. The plastic coverall suit was to prevent these or any other types of contamination.

She surveyed the vent.

The lichen doesn't spore, so I'm safe there. It looks fairly young, so it shouldn't hold too tight. The edges of the pipe are nice and sharp too; I can scrub over that and kinda cut it off the hole.

She started to scrub, separating the lichen.

Hm, even as young as it is, it's really easy to get off. The roots are barely gripping.

When she finished, there was a round slab of lichen that had covered the opening. She rolled it up to throw in the reclamator for an extra bit of charge. The tough chitin that makes up fungal cell walls made it difficult to break down, so the reclamators didn't give much charge for fungal material.

That didn't take long at all. I might be able to get in an extra two jobs this cycle if I keep up this pace.

She backed up carefully and swept the site with her eyes to let the AR glasses see the job was done. A blue light flashed on the peripherals of her vision, indicating successful completion of the task.

She ducked down and grabbed the edges fast as the platform started retreating toward the ground. Once down, she detached the platform and looked to make sure the creep wasn't around. Then, she made her way over to the terminal.

The terminal would only give her her power-chip, or pip, if she returned all the tools and the same task coordinator. She inserted the coordinator, put the tools back in their compartment, and dumped the lichen bio-matter in the attached reclamator. Then, she got her pip. She grabbed one of the other task coordinators on the terminal to replace the broken one and quickly made her way through the crowd, gripping the handle of her stun-baton and looking around for the creep.

I don't see them. Maybe they're waiting for me to get relaxed, or maybe they're gone. I better go a few blocks just to be safe; I can lose them in the crowd.

She faded into the stream of bodies, wary of everyone around her. Once she was sure she wasn't being followed, she leaned against a building and looked for another task on the new coordinator.

Chapter Three | The Suit

Kalan placed a fourth pip, from a fourth job, on the stack in her hand. The rims magnetically aligned together to make one larger cylinder. The number on the face of the top pip changed from 3750 kJ to 15 MJ. The faces were smart surfaces that raised and lowered to show the exact amount of charge contained within the small power cells, and when aligned in a stack, showed the combined charge.

She gripped the stack in her hand excitedly and put it in the inner pocket of her coverall.

Fifteen! I haven't gotten fifteen megajoules in one cycle in forever. It's still early, too, I can grab Sett early and spend some time with her. I should get her a can of air on the way. This is gonna be great!

23

The air was fairly clear because it hadn't rained since before the first task. She unstrapped her face mask and let it hang around her neck. Even with the air as clear as it was, she had to stop herself from taking a deep breath. She needed to regulate her breathing to be slow and shallow, taking in only as much air as was necessary. She hated wearing the big heavy mask, but it was preferable to the wet shuddering coughs that developed from prolonged exposure to the acid rains.

She looked up at the signs, found one pointing toward the yards, where she'd meet up with Sett, and started walking that way. As she did, it occurred to her that she hadn't been checking her equipment between jobs. Her excitement drained into anxiety and her blood rushed from her head. She hastily inspected her suit.

No no no, how could I be so stupid? I always check. The jobs were quick and easy, maybe nothing happened. My arms are fine. Gloves are secure and attached. Boots too. Legs good. Torso okay. My side. There's a tear.

She stuck her hand through a tear in the suit on her left side. Anxiety flowed into panic. She started pacing.

What do I do? What do I do? How long has it been there? How did I not notice?

She felt light-headed, like she was about to pass out, but she couldn't stop pacing. Sitting down felt wrong. She had to keep moving, but she didn't know where to. She ran.

She ran into the first building she saw and into the stairwell. She went under the stairs on the first floor; it was somewhere to be alone without paying for a unit. She paced back and forth, breathing erratically, going back and forth between shaking her hands wildly and gripping the suit over the tear in an attempt to hold it shut.

What'd I do? I ruined everything. I'm gonna have mushrooms growing out of my back, and I'm gonna die, and then Sett's gonna be all alone, and then she's gonna starve, and it's all my fault cause I didn't just check my damn suit! What's wrong with me? How could I forget this?

She paced around for a bit longer and tried to calm herself down.

Stop it! Stop it. It's okay. I mean, it's not okay, but maybe it's okay. Take a look at the hole and see if there's anything there. Like what? I don't know, a mushroom growing out of my back. There wouldn't be a mushroom growing out of my back, that's stupid. Itching. That's it. When Aaron got hit with a cloud, he was itching like mad for cycles. Then he died. Stop, just see if it itches.

She stopped moving and tried to slow her breathing so she could focus all her attention on the area just under the tear.

I don't feel anything. Does that mean I'm okay? How do I know? Would it already be itching or does that come later? Maybe it only itches if I scratch it first. Grr, I don't know! Okay, Stop. I don't feel anything. I'm pretty sure I checked the suit last cycle. Right? Yes, yes. So I just need to sew up the suit. No. A new one. I'll get a new one, and then I'll pretend like none of this ever happened. It'll be fine. Okay. That's it. That's what I'll do.

She let herself sit down for a moment. She sat against the wall under the stairs in the dark, holding her knees to her chest like she did when she was a kid. She sat and breathed. Slowly the world stopped wobbling. Her upper lip was tingly from hyperventilating, but slowly, it also returned to normal.

She got up, went back outside, and found a sign for a market. She numbly followed the signs through the streets until one pointed up. The markets were typically on the fiftieth floor so they'd be closer for everyone no matter what floor they started on.

The building had a lift attached to the outside; the cheapest way to ascend the city. There was a flat charge rate to get on, regardless of how long you rode. The caged platforms spanned the entire side of a building and stuck out a quarter of the way across the street. They could move about a hundred people at once, but at a slow, constant speed; about one floor every thirty to forty-five seconds. One had just left the ground floor, the next one would leave in five minutes but Kalan didn't want to wait. She couldn't wait; she had to keep moving. She jogged into the building and up to the fourth floor.

She focused on a list of tasks in her head, cycling through it over and over to keep herself calm. Get to a market. Find a shop selling clothes with a scrub suit. Buy the suit. Get to the yards. Find Sett. Everything will be fine. Get to a market...

She made her way to the lift gate; the display showed '150 J'. She took out her small stack of pips and twisted the top one to the left; the numbers flashed back to 3750 kJ and then began descending. She stopped when it got down to 200 J; She didn't want it to take the pip in case she needed more than three to make change. She lifted the pip off the stack, which now read 14999.8 kJ, and inserted it into the slot in the door jam. The machine extracted 150 J and dropped it back out with 50 J on its face. She grabbed it, put it back on the stack, and walked through the turnstile.

She was then standing on an open ledge while she waited for the lift to get up to her. She felt an updraft blow through the hole in her side and nervously grabbed it shut. Standing on the ledge reminded her of when she was little. She lived with a group of kids who'd been abandoned. Most parents kicked their kids out when they got big enough to fend for themselves. They'd run through the streets, begging for charge or looking for scraps at the yards to throw in the reclamators. Sometimes, when they found enough charge to ride the lifts, they'd ride them up to the top and drop things off the roofs. While they waited for the lift to come up to their floor, they'd dare each other to jump onto it. Whoever jumped from the highest, won. There were the occasional bruises and scraped knees. One time, her friend, Tenk, broke his leg going for a record. They stopped daring each other after that.

Kalan stepped onto the elevator. She looked around the platform at the various small shops. They were a patchwork of plastic sheets laid on the grated floor with assorted wares spread across them. There were two with tarps on poles to protect from the rain. They'd even sell standing room under them when the rain started. She spotted one with some air cans for sale.

Since I have to buy a new scrub suit, I might not be able to get one for Sett, but I can at least afford one for myself to calm down.

The woman running the shop sat in a crouched position, ready to jump up at any moment. She had tight, twitchy muscles stretched thin over a long, skinny skeletal frame, and loose, leathery skin the color of smoke from an oil fire. It was the tight, efficient musculature of scarcity and chronic over-exertion that most in the city shared. Her left ear was missing, in its place was a small wire cone that contorted to catch sounds in all directions, like a cat's ear. In her right hand, she held a pipe with a stun-baton on the end, like a spear, the other hand was free to make transactions. A cage enclosed the lifts so people couldn't just jump on when at ground level. This made it harder for people to steal from the shops, but every bit of charge mattered, so the vendors always kept a close watch on their merchandise.

Kalan pointed to an air can and slowly handed her a 50 J pip. Without taking her eyes off Kalan, she smeared her bony, arthritic finger over the surface to verify the amount was correct. She nodded slightly. Kalan took the can and walked to the other end of the lift.

It started drizzling. She pulled her hood over her head and looked out over the side, trying to distract herself from her possible infectious demise. She eavesdropped on a transaction going on near her in one of the tented shops. A tall, young man with grey, marble colored skin had a long gash on his forearm that a mender was about to treat. His other arm was prosthetic just below the elbow. The mender was about the same age, with wide, blunt facial features. She wore a one-piece work suit with the sleeves torn off for better movement. She roughly grabbed the man's wrist and tugged it under a glowbe to inspect the wound.

She looked up at him and said, "One megajoule."

He replied, with irritation in his voice, "A whole megajoule? No way!"

"This'll take half a tube of goo to close up. You can always walk around bleeding and try to find a better deal. It's not my problem."

His tone changed to anxiety, "Look, all I've got is 600 kilojoules. Please?"

She held out her hand and with an annoyed look on her face, said, "Pay up."

With his prosthetic, he reached into the pocket of his worn pair of pants and pulled out a stack of pips and handed it to her. The number read '580 kJ'. She scowled up at him, then motioned to his prosthetic.

"How much you got in there?"

"No, come on, I need it to work. Please," he begged. She grabbed his prosthetic and ejected the pip; it read '2 MJ'. She replaced it with a 1MJ pip and gave him back his stack of pips, then gave him an extra pip with 20 kJ on it.

"There. Now sit down, we'll fix the meaty one," she said as she got out some supplies.

"How'd you get this? Mine?" she asked while pouring water over the wound. It was deep, Kalan saw the muscle flinching through the opening in his skin.

He replied between winces, "Refinery. Ouch. I got too close to a crusher wheel. A piece of metal stuck on it slashed me open."

She took some tape and loosely pulled the two sides of the cut together, leaving gaps of exposed muscle.

"Is that what happened to old clanky too?" She said snidely, nodding toward the prosthetic.

"No. Well, yeah. It wasn't a piece of metal,though. My sleeve got caught while I was dumping a load of ore; it pulled my arm into the crusher. Same one, now I think about it. The crusher blade sliced right through. Took me 10 cycles in a deep mine to get enough charge for the new arm. Then they tell me I gotta keep feedin it charge just to make it keep working. I might not've gotten it if I'd known that."

Prosthetics used charge to power them. So, someone would have to get extra pips to keep them running. The benefit of having a working limb usually outweighed the extra work, though. Without them, most would starve.

"At least it's below the elbow. Don't have to worry about charge for the joint. Probably saves you a lot," the mender commented.

She picked up a small tube with a black, oily-looking substance in it. It was usually called goo or bio-goo. Kalan didn't like the stuff; it always reminded her of the sticky ooze that dripped off the bottom of some mushrooms. She thought that's where the goo came from.

It was actually made up of trillions of nano-robots. They were the key to combining biological and technological systems; their main function was to communicate between the two. With the nano-bots, a prosthetic understood the nerve impulses from the brain and the nerves understood the digital signals from the machines. They were also capable of self-aligning; they could form a variety of shapes and densities. Their programming was such that they did whatever was necessary for whatever they were in contact with. So, for a prosthetic, they would form a sort of adhesive, attaching the living cells to the prosthetic and translating between them. Another function was acting as surrogate cells, like with the cut. As the mender poured the black liquid into the cut, the nano-bots attached to cells of the skin and determined that it was trying to repair itself. Then, the bots worked together to pull the skin back into the correct position, closing the cut while the new skin cells formed. The new cells would replace the nano-bots. As the bots were replaced, some would fall away and some would get absorbed into the body and start floating around, doing whatever was necessary. They were small enough that they used the electromagnetic fields permeating the air to keep operating.

Since the nano-bots had been in use for a long time, loose bots permeated everything and everyone, but not in quantities to where they could heal a cut on their own. They had no propulsion systems, which meant they couldn't direct their path, but they floated through everyone's body doing random tasks to help. They supplemented the immune system and fought infections, which kept the city from succumbing to catastrophic outbreaks.

Kalan watched the bio-goo pull the sides of the cut together while the mender pulled the tape off and said, "There you go, you'll be fine in a few cycles. Maybe think about looking for a new job. They're all dangerous, but this one doesn't seem to like you."

The man cradled his freshly fixed arm, thanked her, and walked away, ignoring her comment about finding more agreeable work.

Kalan decided to use the filtered air can while she waited for her floor. The cans were the only respite from the acrid taste of the rainy street air. She put the mouthpiece around her nose and mouth and inhaled deeply while pressing the release button.

It felt like every cell in her lungs were bursting at once. She dropped the can and started coughing violently, collapsing to the floor on her hands and knees. Her vision went dark from the effort and lack of oxygen. The coughing fit grew until she vomited, which calmed the convulsions, but her body was shaking from the exertion. Her vision started coming back in pulses with her heartbeat. As things came back into focus, she saw the grated floor in front of her, and there in the vomit she'd just produced, she saw several small mushrooms and other fungal material. This sent her into a full panic.

She scrambled backward across the floor, then got up and ran to the other end of the platform, bracing herself against the cage wall nearest the building. She wanted to get off the lift as quickly as possible. Catching her breath, she looked up to see everyone staring at her, including a familiar form; at the opposite corner of the platform stood the creep. She refused to wait any longer for the lift; she climbed the cage and pulled herself up onto the next level and ran through the exit gate into the building. As she did, she looked back to see the creep moving toward the building after her.

She ran as fast as she could, her lungs still burning from the violent upheaval, up the last few flights of stairs to the fiftieth floor. She made her way outside onto a walkway and followed the signs to the market. She didn't stop running. She couldn't stop running, her panic wouldn't let her again, no matter how much her lungs begged her to. She didn't know what the creep wanted with her, but she knew it wouldn't be good, and she wanted to get as far away from the mess she made on the platform as possible.

She made her way into the market hall. The entire floor of the building was one large room, with tents and shops set up in no discernible order. She made her way toward the middle, away from entrances where the creep might come in if they were still following her. She kept moving, keeping an eye on the doors, moving through the aisles of tents, using them to hide. After twenty minutes without seeing them, she decided it was safe.

After another thirty minutes of searching, she saw a scrub suit hanging in the back of a tent with a large older man sitting on a stool at its entrance. He had an unkempt white beard and dark, almost black skin with age spots a few shades lighter. There was a big grin on his face, showing his incomplete set of teeth. He wore an old pair of brown pants and a long, sleeveless tunic. His right arm was prosthetic all the way up to the shoulder. It reached up over his neck and wrapped around his ribs, just under his chest. It was a much more complicated model than the one the man on the lift had. The end of it, where his hand would be, had what looked like a sewing machine attached to it. He wore it in a sling. Kalan thought it might be to cut down on the amount of charge he'd have to feed it.

The seller saw she was interested in his scrub suit since she was wearing one herself, and because she was staring right at it. The big man waved at her, calling her over, "Hey, Friend! Come over, try it out. It's the only one on this floor, can ya imagine? Name's Old Jim. On account o' me bein' old; and Jim. Ha ha."

"I- I got a tear in mine, I need a new one. How much is it?"

"Just a tear? I can sew that up for ya, no problem. 200 joules," the vendor said through his big grin while brandishing his sewing hand up like a trophy.

"Cave in down in the mines. Took out me whole arm. I was trapped for half a cycle, can ya imagine? They just kept diggin' around me. Thought I was dead on account o' me not sayin nothin'. I'd been knocked out, ya see. Finally, I came to, and they decided to help, as long as they gotta keep any ore they found on top o' me. Can ya imagine that? Anyway, then I got this off a guy at the salvage yards.

Great deal, too. Of course, it was cause it barely holds its own weight. He didn't tell me that part, though. I had to find out on me own when I gooed the thing to me shoulder. Ha ha! Well, it all worked out fine 'cause I just tied it up in this old sling and, hey, it came with a new job! Now I can sew anything. Better than getting buried in the mine, eh?

"He said it was an old med-cal arm, from when they used to sew people closed like a pair o' pants. Can ya imagine that? People walkin' round with string in 'em like some kinda doll. Oh, I guess they didn't always have that goo stuff, though, huh? Here, let me take a look at that tear."

Kalan stood, stunned by the man's explosion of a personality, then uttered shakily, "uh, no. No, I'd really rather have a new one. I don't want to just patch this one. Really, thank you, but how much for the new one? Is it okay? Does it have any holes or anything?"

Old Jim's energy dropped a tad, "Nah, it's fine. There's nothin' wrong with it. It'll be a lot more expensive though." His grin faded a bit as he looked Kalan over, trying to decide what to ask for. Then, with a bit of a glint in his eye, he said, "I'll tell you what; how's about you give me that old suit and 2 megajoules. And that little old tooth you got hangin' round your neck."

I forgot about the tooth. I guess it's probably not worth anything, and I really need that suit. He's acting funny, though.

"Sure, here you go," she said taking off the tooth and handing him a 2 MJ pip with it. Old Jim took the payment, then reached behind and grabbed the new suit. Kalan took it and thoroughly inspected it before changing into it.

"Nice doin' business with ya. Come again! Ha ha!"

Kalan felt his laugh had a sinister hint in it now. She wondered if she'd just been deceived.

I needed this suit, though. There was nothing else I could've done. It's over now. I'm safe. I still have enough charge for a unit, so that's good. At least this cycle's almost over.

She left the market and made her way to the yards to pick up Sett.

Chapter Four | The Yards

Sett sat in the middle of the street at the edge of the salvage yards, waiting with a small crowd of people. The pile of trash pressed against the walls of the buildings and slowly flooded the streets. It was mostly scrapped construction materials too heavy to move or too large to fit in the reclamators. New trash dropped from above regularly, feeding the slow refuse cancer spreading through the streets. The salvagers looked for anything useful they could sell, or anything small enough to fit in the reclamators to get them some charge.

Someone appeared at the top of the pile with a glowing green mohawk on an otherwise bald head. Sett smiled. She got up, looked around at the others waiting on the ground, then ran into the pile and started climbing.

"Sett! Wait for the cycle thunder. It's dangerous," shouted one of the older salvagers on the ground.

"It's fine. Look, Spatt's already up there. I don't wanna miss all the good stuff," she yelled over her shoulder while she climbed.

When she got to the top, she saw the rest of the usual group of glow-punks looking through the trash. She loved their chaotic playfulness and tried to join them whenever they showed up.

"Hey, Monkey, how you been?" Spatt asked Sett. The glow-punks called her Monkey because she was small and gangly and good at climbing things. They used her infatuation with them to get her to climb up and get things they couldn't reach.

"I'm good. Haven't seen you in a few cycles; been doing anything exciting?" Sett loved listening to their misadventures.

"Nah, just the usual. We got away from a bot that wanted us for breaking a door lock. It didn't stand a chance," Spatt said with a sly grin. Sett's jaw dropped.

"A robot? Did you see it? How big was it? How'd you get away?"

Everyone knew that robots came for anyone who tried to manipulate the locks on the unit-doors or the task terminals, and everyone knew that no one got away from them.

Spatt ignored her and called down to the other glow-punks. "Hey, mushroom heads, you find anything good?"

"Yeah, I found your bollocks. Come down here and get 'em," came the reply from Canner, the taller of the four, wearing a transparent long coat with glow-wire over his shirtless torso. They were scavenging in a pit below Spatt and Sett. Spatt laughed and made a rude gesture with her arm, then slid down a girder to their level. Sett hesitated. The scavenger on the ground had been right to warn her, the cycle thunder was coming, and it was safer on top of the pile rather than down in a pit.

"C'mon, Monkey, what're you waitin' for? Yer missin' out on some primo junk," Spatt called.

Spaz it! She thought, then expertly ran down the steep girder and jumped down next to Spatt. Just as she landed, the cycle-thunder started. She felt the tremor first, coming from off in the distance, building quickly. Then, just at its climax, all the hairs on her body frizzed and stood on end. The tremor faded; the first of fifteen, each faster and closer together. She looked around the pit and braced her feet, hoping the pile wouldn't collapse in on them. At the last tremor, a small amount of debris from the other side rolled down the wall of the pit.

Made it.

There was a long moment of settling stillness, then a far off clap of thunder punctuated the experience with finality. This sequence happened every twelve hours, marking the end of one cycle and the start of another.

Sett heard the others on the ground climbing now that it was safe. She looked around at the punks. Spatt and Canner were wrestling over a scrap of metal. Jaks was jumping up and down on a pipe, trying to dislodge it from the surrounding junk. His boot slipped off the pipe while coming down, smashing his face into it. He rolled over laughing, blood from his nose covered his face. Puke's legs stuck straight up in the air while the rest of her body was inside a hole she was investigating. Izzy, who had a glowing tattoo of a monkey's head covering the left side of her face, looked over at Sett and rolled her one organic eye at Puke's and Jaks' antics. Sett giggled back.

An hour of rummaging later, a troop of monkeys showed up on the rim of the pit. They searched the yards for discarded food. The small animals lived off the mostly rotten bits of fruit rinds that showed up in the trash. Sett liked watching the monkeys, they reminded her of the glow-punks with their mischievous play. She also liked that her nickname was Monkey. It made her feel like she was one of them; like it was her punk name. Canner, however, was not fond of their furry visitors. A monkey bit him once, and ever since he hated them. He picked up an empty water can and yeeted it at the animals, hitting one on the back of the head. The troop scattered, screaming as they went.

"Yee-ah, got it! Didja see that?" he shouted.

"Hey! We coulda deposited that. Leave 'em alone, they ain't hurtin' no one," Jaks scolded.

"Tell that to my ear. One o' them nearly bit it off? Them's vicious little bastards."

"Yeah, I remember. I was there, you were trying to force it to sit on your shoulder. It just wanted to get away from ya. Just like everyone else, eh? Ha ha!"

They started wrestling around, play fighting. Jaks scrambled up the side of the pit and started throwing things down at Canner and jumping around like a monkey to mock him. Canner climbed up and tackled him. They continued wrestling on the edge of the pit. Spatt and Izzy cheered them on from below.

Sett went over to help Puke dislodge a long piece of metal.

"Did you really get away from a bot for breaking a door lock?" she asked.

"Nah, don't listen to Spatt. We found a unit with a broken lock and were crashing in it when we thought we heard something, so we ran. It was probably just someone else lookin' for a room. She likes to think she's a badass," Puke replied while she casually sat back and started picking at her peeling skin; she never wore a shirt, so she was constantly being exposed to the acid rains. Her skin was a splotchy slate grey.

Sett was a little disappointed. She liked to think the glow-punks were every bit as exciting as Spatt pretended they were. If she didn't have Kalan to take care of her, she'd go with the punks. She figured she'd leave and go with them at some point anyway, but she couldn't leave yet.

Jaks and Canner's wrestling had turned into a tussle. Jaks had thrown a soft punch that landed hard on Canner's eye, who then started getting more aggressive. He started shoving Jaks toward the edge.

Spatt called up, "Alright, that's enough."

Izzy yelled, "Knock it off, one of you're gonna end up spazzing out."

Sett and Puke turned to look up at the fight. Canner hit Jaks hard in the face, spinning him around. Jaks lost his footing and started falling face-first into the pit. Sett saw the panic in Jaks' eyes and Canner's hand grab Jaks' arm. There was a muffled pop and a spark jumped between Canner and Jaks.

Jaks fell forward into the pit, unconscious, and Canner fell backward up top.

"Dammit, I told you," said Izzy. She sighed, picked up a long piece of plastic, and poked at Jaks.

"Canner. You dead?" laughed Spatt while she climbed up.

Izzy and Puke flipped Jaks on his back and opened his vest. Puke put her ear against his chest while Izzy poked his face trying to wake him up.

"Canner! Canner, wake up. Canner, no!" Spatt screamed from above.

Puke, Sett, and Izzy looked up. Puke said, "He's fine. Come on," referring to Jaks. They all scrambled up the side of the pit. Spatt was angrily beating on Canner's chest.

"He's fried," sobbed Spatt.

"You mean, he- he's dead? But- how?" Sett stuttered.

"He must've grabbed him right when he spazzed. Dammit, Canner, you idiot. I told you. I told you."

Sett didn't know what to say or feel. She'd never seen anyone get fried before. She'd heard about

49

it, but didn't really understand it. She knew never to attack someone because if they got too scared they'd spazz out, and if you were touching them when they did you'd get shocked and most likely end up dead.

What really happened was that when someone had an intense spike in adrenaline, the nano-bots scattered throughout their body interpreted it as an attack. They'd consume all the chemical energy around them, convert it to electrical energy, and release it; effectively turning the person into a living stun gun, but on a deadly level. The process left the nano-bots destroyed and the person exhausted, sometimes unconscious.

If the person who spazzed actually was being attacked and was in contact with their attacker, the attacker was almost always killed. The positive side effect was that physical violence was almost unheard of in the city. The mortal risk was too great.

Sett sat to the side, feeling numb, while she watched the rest of the punks strip Canner's body and divide up his few belongings. Puke took his transparent long coat and put it on, then kissed his hand and went back down into the pit. Sett saw her wiping tears from her eyes as she left. The others finished stripping the body, taking what they wanted, piling what they didn't to the side to sell or deposit later.

Spatt came over and sat down next to Sett.

"You doin' alright, little monkey?"

The name felt different now. In her mind, she saw Canner throwing the can at the troop of monkeys.

"How can he be dead?" she said.

Spatt leaned back on her hands and answered coolly, "It happens. Nothin' you can do about it, you know? We just gotta keep movin'. Don't let anything slow you down, as long as you're movin', you're not dyin'. That's what Canner always said."

"Why was he called Canner, anyway?"

"That's where we found him. He tasked in the water cannery. He was the only one of us who ever tasked. He'd steal scraps of metal from the shears and toss them out the building vents for us. Then, we'd all take the charge and crash in a unit with as much food as we could get. They eventually caught him and he ran. Then, we all just stuck together. We never ate as good after that, but nothin' lasts. He'd say that, too. Nothin' lasts. It's kinda our motto. Keep movin', nothin' lasts. Don't forget your eye."

"Huh?"

"Ha ha. Izzy. She kept losing her prosthetic eye. Drove him crazy 'cause we'd have to go back and look for it all the time. Come on. We gotta dump him. We'll get a giant charge load for his body and we'll go get all the food we can stomach, then pass out in a unit with a mattress. Just like we used to. For him. Come on."

Spatt got up and pulled Sett to her feet. They walked to the edge of the pit and looked down to see how Puke and Jaks were doing. Jaks was sitting up but still looked asleep. Puke was gathering their smaller piles of scavenged materials onto a tarp.

Spatt called down, "How's he doing? He gonna make it?"

"Him? He's fine. There's not a lot here. Waste of a cycle if you ask me."

"That's okay. Get him up. We're gonna go dump Canner. Bring the stash."

Spatt and Izzy carried Canner's body while Puke carried the tarp full of junk over her shoulder. Jaks shuffled behind them still dazed and Sett trailed behind. Her shoulders hung limp and she stared blankly at the ground in front of her while she walked.

It happened so fast. I didn't even see it; and that's it? That's the end? He's just gone? Spatt said we're just supposed to keep moving, but why, if that can happen to any of us any time?

She hugged herself while she walked. She looked up and saw they'd reached the reclamator and were putting his body up to the chute. She quickened her pace to catch up.

As she approached, Jaks collapsed in a heap against the wall. The others slid Canner's body down without a word. After a few seconds, and some shrill chirps from the terminal, five pips dropped into the dispenser. They each had ten megajoules on them. Sett had never seen so much charge before.

"Well, he was good for something, huh? Musta been all them teeth. He always had good teeth.

They're worth a mega each, you know," Spatt said. "Come on, we're gonna eat so good."

"Oh, good. I've never been so hungry. Puke, help me up," Jaks moaned.

They started walking toward the food dispensaries. Sett hesitated.

"You comin, monkey?" Izzy called.

Any other cycle she'd have given anything to go with them, but right now all she wanted was to stay and wait for Kalan.

"Um, no. I can't, I gotta wait for sis. I'll see you next time," Sett replied.

"Okay, you don't know what you're missing though. Here, take the rest of the junk, we won't need it. Later," Puke said as she handed her the tarp. Then they left her there. Alone.

She dragged the tarp over to the reclamator. She stood and stared into the chute for a few minutes, then slung the tarp over her shoulder and walked away. It didn't feel right to throw the junk on top of his body. She emptied the tarp in a different reclamator, then went back to the edge of the yard and sat on the end of a girder to wait for Kalan.

Every minute felt longer than the last. She kept imagining if it were Kalan who'd been killed instead of Canner. She didn't know what she'd do.

Finally, she saw Kalan walking through the smog. She jumped down and ran over to her and threw her arms around her waist.

"Hey. Nice to see you too. Everything okay?" Kalan asked.

Sett sniffed and smeared a tear on Kalan's new suit and said, "Fine. You're late."

"Yeah, sorry. It's been a weird cycle. Let's go get some food and find a unit to crash in."

They walked toward the dispensary in silence.

Chapter Five | The Dispensary

Sett and Kalan entered the dispensary in silence. It was another large open area on a floor near the middle height of the city, similar to the market. The layout was much more ordered, however. An enormous pipe ran across the ceiling from one end to the other, splitting off at regular intervals to smaller pipes that ran down near the floor. From there, smaller tubes fed into large cones, which fed into waist-high boxes. A thick layer of dust covered the tops of the pipes and boxes. Acid-rainwater trickled into the room through the walls and along the bottom of the pipes and dripped from the machinery.

Monkeys ran back and forth across the tops of the pipes and along the machinery looking for any food to steal. Some would crawl around on the floor under the lowest pipes between the boxes, grabbing scraps that fell to the ground. They'd also reach around and grab food right when someone opened a box to get their meal. It was chaos.

Crowds bunched up around the boxes furthest from the dripping. It was easy for pickpockets to operate since anyone at the dispensary would have some charge on them. Knowing this, people shoved their way to the boxes, trying to get their meals first; there were no queues or orderly processes. The goal was to get in and out as fast as possible.

Sett and Kalan went to a corner box near the wall where the main pipe came into the building. It was far enough away from the main pipe to be somewhat dry but close enough that it was often avoided. They'd be able to get their food without having to fight any people. Sett went up to the box while Kalan stood behind her facing the other way to block anyone from getting too close. Sett put in a pip and waited for the door to unlock. She slid her foot across the ground underneath the box in case there were any monkeys lying in wait, then opened the door and pulled out two bowls of rice and two cans of water. They made their escape, holding the food close.

They went out onto a metal walkway and sat with their legs dangling over the side. They ate their rice while looking out over the city, watching the signs crawling over the sides of the buildings, and occasionally disappearing around the corners. It was like a slow dance of lights through a midnight fog.

Sett wanted to talk about Canner, but she didn't want to tell Kalan what happened. She knew Kalan wasn't too fond of the glow-punks. It wasn't that she didn't like them, or thought they were dangerous, she just preferred the stability of a task out of a terminal to hoping to find something to sell. Scavenging at the yards was one thing, there was always a steady stream of rubbish to go through, but the punks didn't spend too much time in any one place. They got bored and moved on, preferring to do as little work as possible, even if that meant they'd go hungry or have no unit to sleep in most of the time. Sett didn't think Kalan would want her following them around.

Sett thought, *I would have gone with them if they'd asked before Canner got fried. I wanted to even after that. But I can't leave Kalan and I don't want to. Can't I have both? What would happen when the punks wander out of the mushroom district? Kalan wouldn't want to leave, she loves it here, and she loves scrubbing; more than any other task anyway. Maybe I could convince her to switch to spraying the buildings. It's kinda like scrubbing, just with poisonous paint. She'd never go for it.*

Kalan was trying to make sense of her cycle without actually thinking about it. Even picturing the mushrooms on the lift for a moment made her shoulders tense up. She hadn't started eating, she just stared out over the landscape.

Kalan thought, *What'll happen if I did get hit with some spores? Sett's tough, but I don't think she can make it on her own yet. Do I tell her? No, I can't. I don't even know if anything's wrong yet. I can wait a few cycles. If I start feeling wrong, I'll tell her. What then though? It's not like I'd be able to get better. And even if there's nothing wrong now, eventually something's going to happen to me. I need to try to make sure she'll be okay without me.*

Sett noticed Kalan hadn't started eating. She was already halfway through her own rice bowl. She slowed down so Kalan could catch up.

Sett thought, *She's always forgetting to take care of herself. She's gonna forget to breathe one cycle and I'm gonna have to be the one to remind her. I know she thinks she's taking care of me, but I don't think she'd make it without me. I don't want her to have to, either. The punks are fun but I feel safe with Kalan. It's always been the two of us. I remember when she told me she wanted to leave the group of kids we grew up in. I was so worried and hurt that she'd leave me, but she never even considered leaving without me. And here I was thinking about joining some glow-punks cause they tell jokes. No. I don't want to leave her. Someone's gotta look out for her. I'll make sure she'll be okay as long as she's with me.*

Kalan took a bite of her rice. It was stale. It didn't usually have much of a flavor, but this was like the opposite of flavor. She forced herself to keep eating. She saw how Sett always watched her eat to make sure she had enough. She knew Sett felt like she was the one taking care of her, but she knew she wasn't ready.

Kalan thought, *Even back when we were in the group she was always trying to take care of everyone, but she was too young to be the leader. No one ever listened to her but me. I was getting too old for the group but I didn't want to leave her there. The group was getting too big, there wasn't enough to go around. I could tell it was gonna collapse soon. It would split into a few smaller groups, and there'd be a few kids that'd end up alone. I couldn't let that happen to her. We had to leave, and I'm glad we did, but it's been hard since then. I guess it was hard while we were in the group too. Everything's always so hard. Never enough time to rest.*

Sett finished her rice and started chewing on the spoon; both the spoon and the bowl were edible, made of compressed rice. She liked the spoon best, but she needed it to eat the rice, so she always had to wait until she finished to start on it. She watched Kalan get through her meal mechanically. An image of Jaks falling backward, and then of Canner's body falling into the chute flashed in her mind.

Sett thought, *What if that had been Kalan? What if she falls off one of those platforms she works on? I need to get her to stop being a scrubber. We can make it if we both scavenge. Maybe we'd have to sleep in a hallway every now and then, but we could take shifts. It could work.*

Kalan cracked open her can of water and took a sip.

She thought, *This is stale too. How can water go stale? Maybe my tongue's messed up from the mushrooms, or maybe they really did get me. Too many weird things happened this cycle. I need sleep. I need to stop scrubbing; it's just too dangerous. I can't die and leave Sett alone. Maybe we could both scavenge, we might be able to manage if we work together. No, scrubbing pays too well. It can be dangerous sometimes, but so is everything else. I could get cut on something at the yards, or the piles could collapse on me. At least I know scrubbing. This was just a weird cycle. I just need sleep.*

They both finished their meals and sat in silence for a bit.

"Let's go find a unit. Maybe we'll get lucky like last time and find one with a mattress," Kalan said.

"That was nice. We hadn't found one of those in a while. I slept so good. Until your alert woke me up, that is," Sett replied.

"Don't worry. I got a new one. No alarms."

Kalan paused, and then said again, "don't worry."

They wandered the buildings and eventually settled on a unit without a mattress pretty close to the yards. Sett spread out the tarp on the concrete floor, and they huddled together in the dark.

Kalan checked the new task coordinator one last time.

No sign of the 575th floor, and no alerts set for anything else. Let's try to really sleep this time.

She tapped off the coordinator and rolled it across the room. She snuggled around Sett and closed her eyes, trying to sleep.

Chapter Six | The Confrontation

"Aaaaagh! I thought you said you got a new one!" Sett yelled over the echoing sound of the task coordinator alert. It woke them up just after the next cycle thunder.

"I did. I don't know what's going on. Where is it?" Kalan tried to see where the device was whenever the strobing light came on while she crawled around grasping with her hands. She found it and turned it off. She investigated the task coordinator while Sett berated her for interrupting her sleep.

"If this is a new one, then why'd you set another alert? These shocks are not good for me, you know. I could wind up like..." She trailed off, remembering she hadn't told Kalan about Canner or what happened.

Kalan barely heard her. She found that same task again.

575th floor; but I know I didn't accept it. What's going on? I couldn't have grabbed the same coordinator. I know I didn't.

Her brain caught up with what she heard, pulling her attention from the device.

She turned and said, "Wait, what? Wind up like who? Did something happen?"

"No, it's fine. Don't worry about it. Hey, did you know a tooth is worth a whole megajoule? Crazy, right? Anyway, I'm going back to sleep. Make sure that thing doesn't go off again or I'll turn it into a prosthetic eye for you," Sett said hurriedly while pulling the tarp over her and turning toward the wall.

"No, something happened, I can tell. Wait, a megajoule? Really?"

"Yeah. I mean, that's what I heard. Why, thinking of reclamating your teeth?" she chuckled, relieved her deflection succeeded.

That's why he wanted the tooth. He did rip me off. Well, I guess I didn't need it, and I got what I wanted. Not like I'll ever find him again, anyway.

Sett was pretending to sleep, and Kalan decided to let her. Kalan's own sleep was unrewarding again.

I feel like I haven't slept in three cycles. I'm not tired, just... restless? These dreamless sleeps are strange. Everything's just black and still. So still. Like I'm not even breathing. What is happening to me?

She got ready and made her way through the building to the stairwell. This one was lit similar to the last, with cascading lights, but instead of one long strand hanging from the ceiling, the lights were stuck to the wall, circling the inner screw. She leaned against a wall on a landing above a group of older kids messing around. They passed an air can to each other and laughed as they threw things down the center of the stairwell, watching them fall. She closed her eyes for a minute and breathed in the chalky acidic air, letting the echoing sounds of the stairs calm her back to normalcy. Afterward, she took out the task coordinator and looked for a job.

It's gone again. Was it really there, or am I going crazy? 575th floor? Sounds crazy. How high would that be? You'd be in the Cloud. Doesn't matter, it's gone. What else is there? Here's one, it's pretty high paying, a lot of scrubbers'll be looking to get to it first, but it's close. I can get it if I hurry.

She hung the coordinator on her harness and jogged down the steps past the kids. The drumming of heavy rainfall aggressively pummeling the ground reverberated through the walls as she reached the last set of stairs. She pulled on her mask and hood in preparation while she descended.

Now we'll test out how water-proof the new suit is. It's coming down hard.

The streets were packed with people coming up from the mines, wading through the accumulating water in the street. She fought her way through them, focusing on getting to the job before anyone else. She didn't like being rough, but she was also fighting her own anxiety about recent events. She needed the distraction.

By cutting through several buildings, she avoided the worst of the crowds and shortened her journey. She hoped it was enough to get her there before the other scrubbers. When she emerged onto the street again, the rain had subsided. The job was on the next street, which she could see was mostly empty. She burst through the last of the pedestrians toward her goal and saw the empty terminal. *Made it.* Then, she noticed someone she recognized in front of her. Old Jim, the clothing seller. He saw her and his face twisted into a scowl.

He dropped the tarp he was dragging behind him and walked over to her, shouting, "Hey, you! No one cheats me. Gimme my suit back."

She stopped and called back, "I cheated you? You cheated me. I found out that tooth was worth a whole megajoule."

"That tooth wasn't worth a millijoule. It musta been some kinda fake. Gimme my suit."

A fake? My tooth? What does that mean?

Her head began to swim again. She stepped back to get a better footing to avoid collapsing.

Old Jim grabbed her by the collar and tried to wrestle the harness off her. Kalan, jostled out of her shock, pushed him off and ran down the street. She turned down an alley, right into a fallen walkway blocking her path. She turned around to see Old Jim brandishing a stun-baton, blocking her escape.

"There's nowhere left to run. Gimme me suit back and I won't stun ya stupid," his previously jovial tone came out gruff and dangerous.

"Look, I don't know what happened. It couldn't have been a fake tooth."

Old Jim slowly moved closer, "And how do you know that, eh? Where'd you get it?"

"It was mine, it fell out last cycle just before I gave it to you."

"You expect me to believe that? Nevermind, gimme my suit!" Old Jim rushed forward and jammed the stun-baton into her stomach.

Nothing.

She flinched from the blow and the anticipation but felt nothing. They both heard the crackle of electricity arcing between the electrodes, but it wasn't conducting through her like it should.

Taking advantage of the confusion, she jammed her own baton into his shoulder. There was a loud pop and the old man collapsed against the wall, convulsing. She ran without looking back; through buildings, up stairs, over walkways, turning away whenever she saw crowds of people that would slow her down. She wanted to get far away from him, from what he said. She kept running.

When she finally stopped, she collapsed against the railing of a wide walkway and sat down to catch her breath.

The tooth was fake. My tooth was fake. The one I pulled out of my mouth. How? What does that mean? It means he was lying, that's what it means. It couldn't have been fake, I took it out myself. It's the only thing that makes sense. He scammed me when he took it and he was trying to scam me again. What about the stun-baton, though? It didn't do anything to me. How? Maybe the suit's insulated? I've never heard of an insulated scrub suit, but that has to be it.

She looked around confused. The walls were bare; great smooth monoliths rising into the Cloud.

Where am I? When did I leave the mushroom district?

She grabbed the task coordinator and looked at it.

Of course, job's gone. Someone else must've grabbed it while I was running through the streets like a monkey on fire. Here's one. Not worth much, so it should still be there by the time I get to it. Even if it does, it'll point me back to the mushroom district.

She picked herself up and started back. The walk back into the mushroom district reminded her why she liked it. The bland, empty walls outside were like a desert, and the district a lush forest full of life. Even if that life could kill her, she liked being surrounded by it. She almost felt a connection to it.

She made it to the terminal without incident, got her tools out of it, and made her way to the job site. The streets were unusually vacant, and when she came to the spot to set up the platform, it felt different to her. She leaned the scrub-brush against the wall and got ready to attach the platform.

It's the signs, they're gone. The only light is coming from me, even the mushroom caps are dark. I've never seen that before.

She paused to look around but couldn't see more than a meter in any direction.

I never realized how dark it is without the signs.

She pushed her feelings aside and grabbed the platform, lifting it up to attach to the wall. Suddenly, she was shoved from behind. She collapsed on top of the platform and screamed. As she fumbled for her stun-baton, she looked around in the thick, dark air for her attacker. She saw the creep turn down an alley carrying her scrub-brush.

Something burst inside of her and her anxiety ignited and flared into angry frustration.

Nothing's gone right since this creep started following me. On top of that, I need that scrub-brush; even if I finish the job without it, the terminal won't give me any charge unless I return everything.

She grabbed her stun-baton and ran down the alley. She turned the corner just in time to see a door close. She grabbed the handle. The door swung toward her, knocking hard against her light harness. It flickered for a second as she rushed through the door into an unlit room with a foul odor. The lights from the harness showed the creep standing in front of her just before it died and the door shut, leaving them in complete darkness. She listened for the creep's breath, but she couldn't hear it. She activated her stun-baton, using the arcing electricity to see. The crackling light revealed who'd been ruining her life. Standing in front of her was what looked like a two-and-an-eighth-meter [7 ft] tall human with no face. There was just a blank, head-shaped mound sitting on top of broad shoulders.

Kalan screamed in terror and fell backward, dropping the stun-baton and landing on her back on the cold concrete. A spotlight turned on beside her. Her previous terror was forgotten in an instant. She scrambled away from what she saw, her mouth wide, shuddering in fear. She was staring at her own dead body, cycles old, with a cluster of mushrooms exploding from its eye socket. Its other eye was open, staring into nothing. Its slackened, gaping mouth resting on the ground creating a grotesque expression, frozen, from what must have been a horrifying last moment.

Kalan blacked out.

Chapter Seven | The Monkey

Kalan apprehensively opened her eyes as the haze of unconsciousness faded. She was sitting against a wall with her hands tied together in her lap. In front of her was her own rotting corpse still illuminated by the spotlight. To her right stood the creep; its body was a collection of fungus fibers and roots twisted around each other to form the idea of a human, but there was nothing human about it. It stood eerily still, not breathing or shifting its weight.

Kalan looked around the room. A large crack went up one corner and extended across the ceiling. Water, leaking from the crack, streamed down the wall. The trickling sound echoed around the small concrete cube of a room; its particular vibration made her spine twinge, increasing her anxiety about the situation. The stream fed a giant shelf-mushroom, pooling in it, creating a reservoir for hundreds of smaller mushrooms. Their thin, hairlike mycelium reached over the brim of the shelf, drinking the water and its acidic nutrients. The walls were covered in an assortment of fungi. She only recognized a few of the species, which she found odd, being intimately familiar with the city's mushroom population. Pods of tiny, round caps peeked through the larger ones. That familiar black substance oozed from many of them, forming small puddles on the floor. It was a kaleidoscopic rainbow of life blooming out of nothing but tainted water. Kalan had to reject her feelings of awe and beauty to hold on to her hate for what these things were doing to her.

As she stared at the mushrooms, a small patch on the far side of the shelf-pool moved. A small furry hand reached out from beneath the rogue cluster, and then another. The clump tore away from the rest of the colony with a crunch and rose out of the darkness. The mushrooms were growing from the skull of a small monkey. Its cranium was split open where the cluster emerged. Its eyes had been replaced with old prosthetics that looked like black coins with a bug like sheen across their surfaces. Its lower jaw was missing; in its place was an old voice synthesizer. The unit, larger than the poor creature's features, was grafted onto its skin with bits of wire and small amounts of bio-goo. The light brown fur of the animal was patchy and matted. Other prosthetics were mounted onto its small body to keep it functioning in this hellish existence. Its breathing was shallow and labored; the goo bubbled around the voice box with each painful sounding breath. Kalan felt terrible for the poor animal.

The monkey slowly climbed onto the Kalan-corpse's rib cage and crouched there while observing the living Kalan with its directionless, artificial gaze.

"Where have you been?" a heavily distorted, mechanical voice buzzed out of the voice synthesizer; slow and without emotion. Kalan didn't know how to react or even what the creature meant. She stayed silent, trying to think of something to say.

"You failed to complete your task," came the mechanical voice again.

"What task? What's going on? Where am I? Who are you? Who is that, and why does she look like me?" The questions erupted out of her all at once. She started squirming, trying to free her wrists from the wire. The creep-monster moved swiftly, grabbing Kalan's shoulders and shoving her against the wall. Kalan tensed up and ceased her attempts at freedom, then looked back at the monkey.

After a moment of silence, the mechanical voice spoke again, "Simply put, we are the fungi of the city. You are here because we need you."

"So, what? You tried to make some kind of disgusting fungus prosthetic of me and it didn't work, so you decided to force the real me to help you take over the rest of the city?"

Another awkward pause, then, "No. You are the copy. This is the human we made you from."

Kalan's blood drained from her head and a cold sweat drenched her body. She felt light-headed like she might pass out again. Her brain rushed to deny what she'd just heard despite the evidence in front of her and her experiences in the last two cycles. She had to refuse it. For the sake of her sanity, for her very existence, she had to refuse it. If she refused it, it couldn't be true.

"No! I'm not- I can't be. I'm not a mushroom! I'm human! You're lying!"

"No, we took this human and created a near-perfect copy of it to suit our needs. You are that copy; a tool. A tool we need in order to save ourselves from the humans."

Kalan sat, shaking. Her mind was shutting down against what it was hearing.

The mechanical voice continued, "We do not wish to take over the city. We have never sought conquest. Our kind existed eons before the humans and their boned ilk crawled out of the oceans, and we will exist long after they have obliterated themselves into nothingness. Normally, we don't need to kill, we feed on what is already dead. The humans kill without reason, out of convenience. Which is why we need you. We are being threatened by the humans and must act in order to continue to live within the city."

"That's a lie, you kill all the time. We have to wear masks to protect ourselves from you. The tiniest spore can kill us, eating us alive."

"No. Long ago, maybe, we posed a small threat to humans, individually; but now, the bio-goo destroys us from their bodies, protecting them from any danger. Only an overwhelming dose directly into a human's lungs could kill them, and even that has not happened for several of their generations."

"That's not true, I've heard of it happening. I've known-"

"You've known nothing. You've only existed for three cycles. Your original knew nothing either. Stories she heard. Exaggerated stories of fear from the past."

"Why would people keep telling stories if there were no real threat anymore?"

"Few things endure like fear and fungus. Their entire existence is fear. It's their only means of survival. They fear what hurts them; they fear what might hurt them; they fear themselves and each other; they fear having too little and having too much, but most of all they fear being alone, yet reject any connection to anything at all. They are fear."

"What are you then? You feed on the dead and destroy everything you touch."

"We do not destroy; we create. We absorb the unused and discarded and reconnect it with the rest of the living world."

There was a pause, but before Kalan said anything else, the mechanical voice cut her off, "enough. This conversation is useless. You are one of us and you must do what we made you to do."

"And what is that?"

"Save us. There is a human with great power who seeks to eradicate us."

"I destroy fungus every cycle. What makes them any different?"

"Yes, the human you came from destroyed us, but only small pieces. One mushroom, or a bit of root structure is nothing to us; we reconnect. We endure. We don't care about the scrubbers. They pose no real threat to us. They merely remove us from the places useful to the humans. This human seeks to destroy all of us, every last spore; just to keep us off a few vents and walkways."

"I agree with them. It'd put me out of a job, but I can always find something else to do," she spat with venom at the primate avatar.

"You will be dead either way. Your amalgamated form is deteriorating even faster than the human you came from. Your 'body' will only last three more cycles before you fall apart completely."

Another chill dripped down her body. Her tongue probed the hole where her tooth used to be. She felt it within her. She knew it was true, but she still fought against it.

"The human we seek lives above the Cloud, where we cannot reach. But we hear all. Our roots go deep in the city, deeper than anyone knows. We know of his plot to use a chemical to melt us off the buildings, and then another to prevent us from taking root again."

Above the Cloud? How could anyone live above the Cloud? Nothing can go that high. The 575th floor? Does it really exist?

She'd been in a few of the larger buildings before, mostly as a kid. When one of her friends would get some extra pips they'd find one of the tallest buildings and ride the elevators all the way up to the Cloud to look out over the city. They'd try to look up, but the Cloud was too thick, too dark. Even looking down was like staring into a shadow, she'd barely be able to make out the neon signs speckling the view.

Kalan spoke again, "If they just don't want you to cover the vents and walkways, why don't you just not do that? You're obviously smart enough to take over bodies and make these monsters, just stay away from the human things."

"This form, as well as yours, is an extreme reaction to an extreme threat. To consolidate our consciousness into a central location like this, takes an enormous amount of energy. It is... wasteful. We do not like to be wasteful, and we do not deign to govern and restrict our individual cells and minds like the humans do. Besides, this human's motives are more complicated than just wanting us to... behave. He would seek to eradicate us no matter how benign we were. It is an alien concept to us, but he does this for personal gain and cannot be dissuaded from it."

"How can one man even do what you say, it takes hundreds, maybe thousands of scrubbers just to clean you off tiny spots. Let him do what he wants, he can't make any real difference alone, not to something as big as you."

"Your original did not understand the world above the Cloud, she did not even know it existed. They are not like the humans you, or she, have known. They command legion. Who do you think sends those thousands of scrubbers?"

That's true. I have no idea where the tasks come from. I always thought the city sent them; maybe the terminals. Where else would they come from? This 575th floor?

"This is also of no importance. We created you to kill this man. We made you when we knew he would create a job for a scrubber to go to him. We sent you out to complete the job, but you disappeared. It seems the replication of the human was more perfect than we thought. You retained her memories, her motivations, and her feelings for her human family. We suspect you went back to them, as if nothing had happened, and tried to resume her life; but as we said, you cannot do this. You are not one of them. You are one of us. Your body will rot and you would be just as useless to them as this corpse. You have no home to go back to. You must do as we created you to do. We have given you purpose. You should be grateful, it is something most humans struggle their entire lonely lives to find, and you have it in singular intensity."

Kalan's resolve was beginning to fade.

It's true. It has to be. It explains everything; the air can, the dreamless sleeps, the stun-baton. My body couldn't process those things because it wasn't meant to. I can't go back.

"What- do you want me to do?" she asked, quietly and defeated.

"You will accept the job. Go up, and complete the task he requests. Then, you'll kill him. He is the one driving the attack against us. Once he is gone, our threat will be gone as well."

"Why not just send this thing?" she said, gesturing to the mushroom golem beside her. "Surely, it's stronger than I am. I don't even know if I can kill someone."

"The human wouldn't trust anything but another human. This beast is little more than a walking brute. We had to create it to make sure you came back, and it will make sure you go to the job this time; but it wouldn't be able to get close enough to the man to kill him. And, if others knew we were capable of retaliation, there would be a war. We do not want a war. It, too, would be wasteful. We do not waste, we use everything."

"I still don't know if I can. What if I'm not strong enough? You said this man is powerful."

"Do what the human requests of you. There you'll find all the tools you need to finish the real job."

The monkey-host paused and moved closer to her, the putrid stench of rot and infection was overwhelming.

"I take it, by these questions, that you have accepted your purpose and will perform it?"

"I don't think I really have a choice. Do I?"

"No. You don't. You never did. That is the price of purpose."

"I do have one question. Why me? Or, why her?" she asked. Finally admitting what she felt was true.

"Prosthetics. We needed a scrubber without prosthetics. The bio-goo they use to attach them kills fungi, as we said. You are a very close copy of the human, but you are still fungus. It's also what protected you from the other human's electric attack. Their stun-batons have no effect on us."

The monkey moved closer still. Its tiny hands grabbed the task coordinator and reviewed it.

"Good. The human has put in the request again," it accepted the job and put the device on her lap.

"Take her. Make sure she gets on the elevator this time."

The avatar crawled back to the mushroom-pool and sank back into its position in the canvas of mushrooms. Kalan looked at it all again with new appreciation. She could accept its beauty now; a little anyway.

The faceless creature pulled her onto her feet effortlessly and untwisted the wire from her wrists. It gripped the collar of the scrub suit tight and lead her out into the street to one of the largest buildings in the city. She hadn't ever been in one of them. They had no entrances, despite being ten blocks in diameter and ascending into the Cloud. She never knew what they were for, but she never thought they went above the Cloud.

They walked to a large metal portion of the wall. The creature took the task coordinator and pressed it against the surface. The wall groaned and sank into the ground.

It's a door. An elevator door.

The inside was bright and large. The creature shoved her against the back wall then flung the task coordinator at her as the door rose again. There were no buttons inside, nowhere to put a pip or to tell it how high to go. When the door finished closing, the elevator started moving uncomfortably fast on its own. The inside of the door lit up with bright blue numbers, indicating what floor she was on. When she got to the 30th floor, she decided it was going to be a long ride and sat down with her back against the wall and her arms crossed over her knees. She put her chin on her arms and watched the numbers change. She started to try to process everything that had just happened.

Chapter Eight | The Elevator

I've only been alive for three cycles? What happened then? I remember waking up and leaving a unit with Sett. I dropped her off at the yards... I can't remember anything else. The next thing was waking up the cycle I lost my tooth. That's almost an entire cycle I'm missing. That must have been when they killed me. Her.

How can I remember things from a long time ago, though? I still remember being in the group of kids with Sett and leaving with her, and the one before that one; the one that fell apart. That first group was where I went when the adults left me behind. How can I remember all that? How perfect of a copy am I?

What was different between then and now? There isn't much to compare things to if I've only been me for three cycles and her for so long. Last cycle I was afraid of being eaten alive by mushrooms, now I am one.

Afraid. There's something, I don't remember being so afraid of the mushrooms before. I never thought about quitting scrubbing before last cycle. Maybe that's just because I had a close call, or what I thought was a close call. I guess it was worse than close if they killed me. Her. But still, she wasn't afraid of the mushrooms. She wasn't afraid of anything. She was always sure what she should do. She knew what was safest and did it. Whatever was safest for Sett and her. I remember how much she loved Sett. How much I love her too.

I do remember her being afraid once. It was when we... they... had just left the group and Sett got sick. I... she... was frantic for six cycles. Sett kept coughing and passing out, then she'd be hot, then cold and sweaty. The real Kalan didn't know what to do, she even tried a mender, but he just tried to give her some goo to drink. You can't drink that stuff, it'd just stick your insides together, wouldn't it? I don't know now. The monkey said it kills the mushrooms though.

89

I thought it just stuck things together. She had to leave Sett in a unit and go get more charge and food and water. She was scared the whole time, especially when Sett wouldn't open the door. I always hated that you can't open them from the outside once they're paid for, but I guess it wouldn't work if anyone could just walk in. She almost broke down the door from pounding on it. She was so relieved when Sett woke up and opened it. She must have passed out. Then, when it was all over, and Sett got better, I never slept so good. She... never slept so good.

That fear was different though. She was worried more than afraid. Worried that something would happen to Sett. She definitely wasn't afraid of the mushrooms though. Why was I so afraid? Is it because they killed me? Her? Maybe I still remember being killed somewhere in my head. I don't think you're supposed to be able to remember your own death.

The air in here is stinging my chest, and the light is so intense. I never thought I'd wish for less light.

The monkey said humans were the ones who lived in fear, but she never did; I was the one living in fear. Why do I feel fear at all? The mushrooms don't and I'm supposed to be a mushroom, right? Is that part of the perfect copy too? Why wouldn't they leave that part out, how does me being in fear serve their mission, my purpose?

Purpose. That word. She felt purpose; Sett was her purpose. She'd felt it when she first met Sett. Some of the other kids found her under the stairs in a unit building, crying and alone. She'd been abandoned, like all of us. Her big eyes, magnified by her held back tears, looked straight through Kalan. She knew what she wanted then, she wanted to never see this child cry again. She'd do everything and anything for her. I think she saw herself in Sett. She knew how that felt, and she wanted to stop it from happening again. That's why she took her away when she saw the group collapsing, she didn't want Sett to be abandoned again. Whenever she made those kinds of big decisions, she felt that purpose again. Is that real purpose though? Just to protect something; what about Sett's purpose? If she never finds purpose, what does

91

that mean for Kalan's? If Sett's life ends meaninglessly, does that mean Kalan's was meaningless too? What if Sett's purpose ends up being to protect someone else, and then they protect one other person, and no one actually does anything. It would just be a long line of people pretending at purpose. I don't know if that counts. I think you have to do something for there to be purpose; otherwise, it's just a lie with a nice feeling.

I don't have that same feeling of purpose she felt though; and they said I'm the one with real purpose. I was created for one specific thing. Isn't that true purpose? Why doesn't it feel like it then? Maybe the monkey doesn't really understand humans as well as it thinks it does. Maybe I don't. I've only been playing at being one for three cycles, how much could I really know?

This air is getting thicker, or thinner; whichever hurts more. If I breathe a bit more shallow than normal it stings a bit less. It feels like the elevator's pumping in filtered air. It must be slow or I'd be coughing myself to death.

I have all these memories that I know aren't mine. How do I know if they're even real? I didn't actually do any of these things, she did. She loved Sett; she rescued her; she had a childhood; she grew up. I can see everything she did and feel everything she felt as if I was there. But thinking back on her life, I think we're very different people; if I am a person. What makes someone a person? Their experiences? I barely have any, and most of what I remember as experiences aren't mine. It's like I stole her life. What would the real Kalan have done the last couple of cycles? Would she have cowared on the platform while watching the robots execute someone? Would she have been scared of the mushroom creep chasing her, or would she have tried to confront it right away? What about the tear in the suit, what would she have done? How different could we be if we have the same memories. But I have the memory, or the experience of, her death; or the trauma of it. If she had lived through the trauma, would she have done everything as I did it then? Is the trauma what separates us? Is that what determined my reactions in my life? What if I didn't have the trauma; would I have been a true copy of Kalan? Would I have been as fearless as her?

I feel the same as she did, I think. I remember her feelings. I remember the excitement of little things, like when she found this '0' pip.

She picked up the pip hanging from her neck and ran her fingers over its faces while she probed the real Kalan's memories.

It was when she was a kid; she'd just started living with the first group. There were so many kids. The older ones, who tried to keep everyone safe, were so overwhelmed. They sent the younger children out in gangs to steal what they could and bring it back.

She found a couple of pips on the ground, it was the first time she'd ever held one in her hand. She was so excited. I even remember how much charge was on them, 40 joules. She didn't wait for the rest of her group, she wanted to show the older kids. So, she ran all the way back to the unit building. Then, when she got inside, she saw the elevators. She'd never ridden on an interior elevator before; they were always too expensive, a luxury. She went up to the door and counted out how many floors she had to go and matched the top pip. Then she dropped it in the slot and waited for the door to open; but it didn't, not at first. The pip slid into the change slot. She thought she'd counted right. She shouldn't get any change. She thought maybe the elevator was broken and she wouldn't get to ride it. I remember her disappointment. The feeling of fighting back the tears and how she thought it was stupid to feel that way. Then the door opened. It was amazing. A tiny room all to herself, with little lights running up the walls just for her. She grabbed the pip from the change slot and ran inside.

The door shut quick after her and the elevator went up. Just like this one. She looked down at the pip and then she saw it; the '0' on its face. They weren't supposed to give you back empty pips, but she had one. She kept it, and one of the older kids showed her how to tie some string around it so she could wear it. I remember her slight disappointment when she learned it wasn't all that rare. '0' pips showed up every once in a while; mostly ones spent from a prosthetic, but unit doors and elevators didn't usually redistribute them. She still felt like she had something all her own.

I remember all that, even how it felt; but is that the same as having lived it? Kalan had vivid dreams all the time, but she hadn't actually lived them. Is that the same as what I'm feeling? Was her life like a dream of mine? But now that I'm awake, what does the dream mean for me? I can feel how she felt when I think about her memories. When I think about leaving the group with Sett, I can feel the excitement for a new adventure and the worry of what could go wrong.

Hmm. Excitement and worry. Maybe that's the difference between fear and worry. I never felt excitement in my life, just fear. Maybe fear plus excitement changes the fear; makes it more manageable. Maybe. When else did she feel excitement?

The lift jumping games; those were exciting for her. Until they weren't. Then there was fear. Tenk screamed and cried like nothing she'd ever heard. They all tried to calm him down, but the break was bad. They knew they had to get him to a mender, but they'd just used all their charge on the lift. They picked him up and brought him to one anyway. He blacked out from the pain halfway there. Kalan felt more fear then, fear of losing her friend. She stayed with Tenk while the others begged for charge from passersby. It took them hours before they had enough for the mender. Then, while Tenk was still passed out, the mender poured bio-goo over his leg just below the knee. I remember Kalan thinking it was too far away from the break, but the mender wasn't trying to fix the leg. He pulled out a saw and started cutting Tenk's leg off along the line of goo. Tenk woke up screaming, then passed out again. The mender barely flinched, his one hand just tensed up on the leg when Tenk woke up, to stop him from moving. After he'd cut clean through, he put more bio-goo on the stump and told them to go away. It was another twenty cycles of all of them begging, salvaging the yards, and doing whatever tasks they could before they could get him a prosthetic. They didn't jump onto the platforms anymore, even after he had the new leg. The excitement was gone and there was only the fear, they all felt it. That's why they stopped jumping; the knowledge of what might happen. That matches what the monkey said; that the humans feared what might hurt them.

The number on the door reached 300.

I've never been this high before. The highest was 100. Wait, no, that was her. Now I'm confused again. The memories feel so real, but they aren't mine. I have to deal with that. That wasn't my life. My life is meant for one thing, death.

Does it have to be though? Can I choose not to kill someone I've never met; why would I; just because they told me it was my purpose? They may have created me, but they don't control me. I won't do it. I can make my own choices. I'll do what I want.

What do I want, though? And how can I know what I want if all I have are someone else's memories? Sett. She was in MY life too. I have memories of her that are my own. There may not be very many of them, but they're mine. I do still care for her; but, is that just because SHE cared for Sett? How do I know what feelings are hers and which are mine? Even if they are her feelings, the only thing I've ever actually cared about in my life is Sett.

She let out an exasperated sigh and
on the floor.

Her. Me. What's the difference? Am I just a continuation of her? They said I'm a perfect copy, but how much did they copy? Is her consciousness, her spirit, in me? How much of me is mushroom? Do I owe them for creating me? Do I really have no choice? Should I complete their task just because they created me? What would the real Kalan do? She'd do whatever she had to to get back to her family. Family. I guess the mushrooms are my family more than Sett is. Should I do whatever I have to to protect them? They said they're in danger. My family is in danger.

What about Sett? What do I owe her? Do I at least owe her the truth? Shouldn't she know her Kalan is gone, that she's never coming back? Even if I accept that the mushrooms are my family, I still feel like Sett is my family too. I want to be with her, even if it's only for the short time I have left. What would I tell her, though? That I'm a monstrous copy of Kalan that's going to die in three cycles? Would she accept me then; or would she hate me for what I am? Could I even go back? The monkey didn't say anything about what happens after I kill for them. Maybe they'll let me go if I do what they want. Then I can go back.

The number on the door stopped changing. It stayed on 388, but the elevator was still moving just as fast.

Why does this air hurt me so much? I feel like I'm getting used to the stinging, but it feels like it's getting worse too.

She got up and started pacing around while she continued to think.

I should prepare myself. I've never killed anyone before. Neither had she. What if the monkey was lying though? What if they tried to make a copy and it failed and that's what I saw? How can I be sure? There's the tooth. It came out without any blood. Does that mean I don't have blood? And what about the stun-baton? That could have just been a faulty baton, though. It doesn't prove anything. How can I know for sure?

She sat down, took off one of her boots, wrestled a sharp piece of metal from her harness, and put the edge against her smallest toe, then paused. The weight of the blade on her toe scared her. She wondered if there'd be pain and thought about the pain she felt with the tooth; then, took a quick, stinging breath in, and jammed the edge into her toe. The blade cut easily and smoothly, but there was no blood. She kept sawing in a fervor, there was a little pain, but not nearly what she expected. The metal hit bone and she kept going, it was only slightly tougher than the skin. Finally, she made it through. Her toe dangled from the rest of her foot lifelessly. There was no blood, and she'd sawn straight through the middle of the bone. She cut it off and examined the cross-section.

It looks human enough; but the colors are strange. They're muted, bland; as far as I can tell, anyway; this light is intense, everything looks so strange and crisp. There's no blood, though, there should definitely be blood. When Tenk's leg was cut there was lots of blood.

The realization caught up with her all at once and the toe terrified her. She dropped it and kicked it across the elevator into a corner. She didn't want to believe it, but there was no doubt now. She wasn't human.

Her decision to go back after everything seemed so far away now.

No matter how I feel about Sett, I can't go back. I'm not human. What if I decay into a fibrous mess in front of her? I can't do that to her. I can't go back. It's better if she just thinks Kalan died while out looking for charge. That is what happened. She just got to see her one last time before she was gone. Like seeing a ghost just after someone dies. That's what I am. A ghost. A remnant of Kalan. I'll go back to the monkey after I finish this mission. I'll go back and lay down next to Kalan's corpse and wait for the end. I died there once, maybe I should die there again.

The numbers started changing again. She wondered how much longer she'd have to wait. She didn't like the elevator. It was too clean and too bright. It made her feel exposed. She stared at the toe on the floor.

That's all I am; just a hunk of mushroom waiting to fall apart. How could they create something just to let it live a scared, short life then let it die? It's cruel. They create me just to do what they want, and then discard me? My life isn't even my own then, it's theirs. What makes their lives more important than mine, or Kalan's? Why should I do what they say? Because they created me? Because they killed me? No. I won't do it. I'll just stay in the elevator until it goes back down. What are they going to do, kill me again?

The elevator started slowing down and the numbers flashed '575'. The elevator door descended. Kalan looked out and immediately forgot about staying in the elevator. Awed, she walked out.

Chapter Nine | The Tower

Through the open door of the elevator, Kalan saw a wall of windows overlooking something that hadn't been seen by anyone below the Cloud in living memory; the horizon. She saw the Cloud below, writhing slowly like a black boiling sea stretching out into infinity. In the distance, the peak of a mountain breached the inky depths like the face of a drowning swimmer desperate for breath. Between her and the mountain were several other towers rising from the Cloud, each with a colorful array of solar panels in the shape of a different flower. Having never seen a flower, she marveled at the novelty of the enormous distant sculptures. Their stalks, glimmering panels of glass, reflected the noon sun from overhead. Gliders with long trails of colored silk flew between the towers. Her eyes watered from the brightness of the crisp white sky, but she willed them stay open, lest she miss any details.

"It goes forever," she whispered.

The far off line of the horizon drew her attention.

How does it split like that? Like two worlds meeting for the first time. A world of light and one of dark. Like me. Am I the first to come from the dark to this light world?

She stepped out of the elevator onto thick, plush carpet. The sensation was at once pleasurable and unnerving. She'd only ever walked on concrete and metal grating. She took another step, indulging in the spongy sinking feeling, then she walked across to the glass and put her hands on it.

It's cold, like metal. The air here is even worse. There's probably nothing of the Cloud in it at all. I finally get somewhere that has clear air and I can't breathe it.

Movement behind her prompted her to turn around. Two small metal spheres rolled down the hallway in her direction. They stopped where she'd just been standing, then both started rolling back and forth as if they were dancing. She crouched down and looked closer. There were tiny black needles shooting out of the bottom, just before hitting the ground, then retreating back into the ball.

What are they doing? It looks like goo is coming out and going back in. Are they going back and forth over my footprints? Are they cleaning my footprints? Why? And why would you waste bio-goo cleaning a floor?

She shifted her boot to look under it. There was an imprint in the carpet where she'd been standing, but it didn't look dirty. She tried to poke one of the balls. It rolled backward out of the way and stopped like it was waiting for her to try it again. After a few seconds it resumed its cleaning. The other ball finished the footprint it was working on and moved to the next one.

Are they going to follow me the whole time I'm here?

She shrugged and stood up, noticing the hallway for the first time. It ran along the windows in both directions. To her right, it turned a corner into the tower, to her left it lead into a room. She walked in the direction of the room, then turned around when she heard one of the robots bumping against the glass. It rolled up the window to where she had touched the glass with her hands. She smiled and continued down the hall.

The hallway opened into a luxurious open area as big as twenty units below the Cloud. The windows formed one wall of the room, the rest was a great semicircle of wood panels, each from a different type of tree, stretching twenty meters [22 yards] across. At the back of the room was a waterfall splashing liters of water per minute onto a stone floor. She found the splashing sound somewhat soothing, in contrast to the trickle of water in the mushroom-monkey's lair. In the center of the room was a sunken area surrounded by flowing sheets of silk hanging from the ceiling, rotating around the pit on a track. Inside were what looked like giant misshapen colored glass beads in various colors. The beads were arranged along the outside of the pit with large cushions between them, and a low circular table in the center.

So many colors. They're so beautiful. Everything is colorful here, even the walls. And everything is so bright; the light, it's everywhere. There's even light falling from the ceiling. Why? There's already so much coming in from outside.

Beyond the pit, along the far wall, were bookshelves packed with thick, old-looking books. They were the only things that looked worn or used in the room. Kalan had seen books before. It was rare, but sometimes they would show up in the yards. To her, books were a useless curiosity filled with unintelligible symbols. Reading had been lost below the Cloud, the closest thing were the pictographs of the services or products offered found on the neon signs. Even the task coordinators showed only symbols and numbers, presenting the least amount of information necessary for the user. Books were only useful for trade to some of the more eclectic vendors in the markets, but the values varied wildly even among them.

Sett had found two in the time she'd been scavenging. One like the large ones on the shelves, filled with neat rows of indecipherable symbols, the other was a large thin picture book. She traded the thick book to someone at a market but kept the picture book for herself for a while. The pictures were bright and colorful with small blocks of the rows of symbols on each page.

I remember when Sett was younger, she and Kalan would sit and look through the book trying to come up with stories to fit the pictures.

The books on the shelf all looked the same to Kalan. They were all the thick, unknowable kind.

Why would anyone need so many of the same thing? What's the point; they take up so much space, and how would you move everything in here? This place is so strange. The air is so clear and moist. There's free water just spilling on the floor and free light drenching everything, but it doesn't look like there's anyone here to use any of it. Everything here is wasted. Great, now I sound like the mushroom.

She walked further into the room. There were more of the giant beads, and some smaller beads next to them lined up in front of the shelves. As one of the silken sheets fluttered by, she saw someone sitting on one of the beads, or rather in one of them.

The smaller bead next to them was a different shape than the others; taller and thinner, forming a small table. On top, was a conical glass balanced on its tip. The person was sitting inside the larger bead. The bead, which seemed solid and immovable by its size and apparent density, was actually extremely malleable. It formed into the perfect chair for them. It wrapped around their body, forming armrests and a headrest with just enough support to minimize fatigue and discomfort. Their legs were outstretched and crossed over an extended portion, which nestled around their legs perfectly, preventing them from straining any muscles.

They looked up at Kalan as she came into their view. The section of bead around their head and neck dropped into the rest of the bead as if it suddenly became liquid, freeing their head for movement. As they turned their head, the book they were reading instinctively dropped a bit; the armrests, instead of dripping into the bead like the headrest, just pressed in as if it was a pillow.

They looked at Kalan with wonder and excitement in their eyes, and said, "Well, look at you!

I thought I heard the lift arrive. You must be the, uh, forgive me, um, scrubber, that's it. I must say, you've had me waiting for quite some time. I put that request in yesterday; and I had to renew it at least twice."

The confused and uncomfortable expression on Kalan's face gave the person pause.

Kalan responded slowly, carefully repeating the strange words, "Yester day?"

"Uh, yes, I put the request in yester-"

They were cut off by Kalan's alarmed reaction to something outside the window. A white capsule burst from the top of the mountain in the distance, shooting up into the air. A moment later there was a clap of thunder that shook the tower. She could see the other towers visibly sway in turn from the shockwave. The capsule kept rising into the sky, growing smaller as it broke through the planet's gravitational pull, until finally, it disappeared from view. Kalan stood still, watching the mountain for any other changes, every muscle tense.

The person, who'd been watching Kalan's reaction instead of the capsule, asked, "Have you never seen a shipment launch? They happen every twelve hours. I suppose you wouldn't be able to 'see' them from below, but surely you've heard them."

All at once Kalan understood what she'd just witnessed; the cycle thunder. She turned toward them, still somewhat startled, and mumbled, "No. I mean, I've felt the quakes and heard the thunder, but no one knows what causes it. Do you... know?"

"Well, of course. Everyone knows. It's the shipments. All those refined minerals get packed into containers and shipped off-world. You mean you can actually feel the ship building up speed in the tunnel on the surface? I suppose that makes sense, I can't imagine it's very quiet.

"You see, to get into space, the ship has to be going some astoundingly fast speed, I don't know what it is, I'm not a launch engineer. Anyways, instead of strapping all our valuable merchandise to thousands of tons of explosives, as they did in the old days, we let it build up speed inside a giant electromagnetic tube that's laid out under the city in a huge circle. The ship goes around the track something like twenty times-"

"Fifteen."

"Uh- right, fifteen times. Then, it leaves the track and goes into the launch tube that climbs the mountain where it launches into orbit without having to use a single gram of on-board fuel. It's an amazing piece of technology. It must have cost multitudes to build, but now that it is, the profit margin should be enormous."

As the person gave this lesson, they stood up. The process was one seamless motion, entirely natural and unconscious on their part. The moment their feet moved away from their perch on the bead, the footrest retreated into the main portion just as the headrest had done; like water falling sideways into the bead. As they moved their feet under their body and straightened out their torso to be vertical, the bead supported their back, lifted their body to the correct height to stand, and sunk inward to allow for their feet. Once standing, they closed their book, rested it on the bead-table, and picked up the glass. Then, walked over to Kalan. As soon as they were out of the way of the bead, it dripped into the same shape as the rest of the beads in the room.

"Now, pardon, my name is Marquese Trellis Haverty Vanderson the Third. Uh, that's of the 'Skyrise' Vandersons, of course, not those boisterous 'tower-hopper' Vandersons. I find it so malheureux that we have to share our name with those poubelle. You may call me Marquese Trellis, if you desire. And what, my uh, interesting, friend, is your name?" said Trellis with a flowery bow and many dramatic hand gestures and eyebrow expressions.

Barely understanding what she'd just heard, she replied, "My name- is Kalan?"

After a moment of inquisitive silence, Trellis said, "Kalan? That's it? No titles, no surname, no degrees, no lineage, no guild, no way to differentiate you from any other Kalan that might come crawling out of the refuse chute?

"Well, I suppose that'll do for our purposes today, but I've never heard of such a thing. Now, let's take a look at you, you certainly are a sight. My word."

The Marquese was walking with an odd, flowy gait around Kalan; looking up and down her body, studying her. Kalan stood uncomfortably, while trying to turn to keep him in front of her. Trellis' clothes were strange to her, so while she was being reviewed, she examined him.

He wore a precisely tailored jacket made of lilac-colored velvety fur material with comically large and elaborately embroidered cuffs and lapels. He also wore a pink shirt with frills and charcoal-grey slacks with black embroidery down the sides. His shoes were plum-colored, complimenting his jacket, made of intricately sculpted leather.

For Kalan, the most interesting thing about him was his skin, which was a dense golden bronze color. She looked down at the skin on her hand to see if it was the same color in the saturating light. It was not, it remained the same ashy grey it had always been, only brighter. His hair also caught her attention. It was strands of gold, implanted into his scalp with nano-tech, allowing for on-demand styling. Currently, it was in the shape of an asymmetric swoop, arching several centimeters from the top of his head and backward, ending in a large curl.

Their eyes met when the two finished examining each other, during which, the Marquese kept mumbling to himself, "Remarkable. Absolutely remarkable."

He smiled, raised his glass, and said, "You, madam, are a marvelous sensory experience. Cheers."

He started to take a sip, then abruptly stopped and said, "Oh, my, but I haven't offered you anything to drink. You must forgive me, come come."

He grabbed Kalan by the elbow and dragged her over to the wall near where she'd entered the room. She saw the cleaning ball robots make their way into the room, still busy cleaning footprints.

Trellis pressed on one of the panels; several of them spun around revealing trays of bottles filled with colored liquids, while another panel opened and a curved wooden plank emerged, forming a bar complete with stools. Trellis sat her down.

"Here, have a seat, I'll make you something extra special," commanded Trellis.

He busied himself behind the bar, pouring different amounts of several of the bottles on the wall into a silver canister. Kalan was surprised when he shook the canister inhumanly fast with one hand.

He noticed her expression and said, "Ah, yes, my arm is prosthetic. Most of me is, actually. Can't tell, can you? We Vandersons like to keep things sophisticated. None of those showy, multi-spectrum prosthetics for us. The more realistic, the better."

When he was done pouring the mixture into a glass, he placed it in front of Kalan, who looked down at it and sniffed. Invisible fumes, coming off the liquid, stung her nostrils even more than the air did.

She backed away from it and asked, "What is it?"

"It's a special cocktail I've been developing over the years. Try it. It'll cronch your world," said Trellis with an expectant grin on his face.

Kalan hesitated as she picked up the glass. She wasn't sure if she should drink it knowing what non-acid-rain water tasted like, but she was curious. She lifted the glass to her lips, closed her nostrils from inhaling the fumes, and took a tiny sip. It immediately burned her mouth, and the fumes invaded her lungs as she tried to cough. She dropped the glass on the floor and continued coughing. She remembered the filtered air can and hoped she wouldn't vomit mushrooms here.

Trellis came around the table and slapped her on the back, saying, "Ha ha. I told you. Good, isn't it? I'm glad you like it," completely oblivious to how much pain she was in.

He led her over to the sunken area and down the steps, sitting her onto one of the large pillows. She eventually stopped coughing, but still felt the burned parts of her mouth, lungs, and esophagus. She'd never had alcohol before. There were no crops to produce it below. The only thing that could have been used to create it was rice, but it was only sold cooked from the dispensaries and there wasn't anywhere to house the equipment needed to ferment it, the craft faded from memory.

Once she finished coughing, she noticed the pillow she was sitting on was more of a balloon made of a clear vinyl-like substance. Inside was an aquarium, complete with fish and vegetation. She gazed astoundingly at one of the other similar pillows.

Trellis started speaking while she was lost in the aquatic microcosm, "Now, as much as I'd love to chat with you all day, you do have a job to do. There is this unsightly growth, you see, forming on the outside of the tower, just below the apartment. It looks as though it's trying to destroy my reputation. It's a large fungus, of all things. Just as I've been having my chemists start working on a solution to rid the city of all of its fungi, this monstrosity starts growing right out of the smog. But, I ask you, how would it look if the leader of the anti-fungal campaign had a giant mushroom crawling its way up to his apartment? Terrible, that's how; and then to make things worse, I lose a robot trying to get the thing off."

The monkey was right. He is trying to destroy them- us- all, she thought.

Trellis continued, "You see, before I sent for you, I had one of my robots go out and try to pry the thing off the side of the building."

Robots? He has robots? Kalan tensed, remembering the robots she'd seen a cycle ago.

"Of course, it fell. The things are supposed to be able to handle any task, and the company claims they're intelligent. Ha! Then, of course, they said it wasn't their fault and refused to replace it.

"That's when I decided to seek an expert. That's you, you see. I knew if anyone could do it, it'd be someone from below. Everyone knows you're the best at this sort of thing. Oh, I hope I'm not keeping you from anything important while you're up here dealing with my little problem."

The pause in the onslaught of speech signaled to Kalan that Trellis wanted her to answer, but she didn't know what to say. She was still trying to comprehend what the Marquese had been talking about, and she was also having trouble keeping up with his quick way of talking.

She tried her best to answer, "No, no, I'd be scrubbing anyway, if I was below. I didn't even know there was an above."

"Really? You know, there are those of us, myself included, who wonder about what life is like down there. Along with being the leader of the movement to eradicate the fungus in the city, I'm also the head of the 'Below the Cloud' cause. It's a group of concerned citizens who want to know more about the people who live down there. We contest that it's actually you, those below the Cloud, that is, who provide all our wealth by working in the mines. We hope to make things better for everyone below the Cloud. We're still a small group, but with you as a representative from below, we could start to make some real change. We'll discuss it afterward."

Kalan became lost in a fantasy of uniting the worlds below and above. She could see Sett getting to grow up in a place like Trellis' apartment instead of in a different unit every cycle, struggling to scavenge enough charge to survive. She saw herself showing Sett what she'd seen.

All this light, the strange animals, so many books for her to look at, even the floor here is soft.

She glanced down at it and saw her boot, remembering the toe. The fantasy shattered when she remembered what she was and how long she had left.

That would have been nice, but I can still get back to her. I have to stay focused on that.

Trellis lifted his arm and made a waving motion, then continued talking, "Now, it truly is time for you to get to work, I don't want to take up too much of your time."

A robot, like the ones in the street, walked in from the hallway and stood right behind her. It was holding scrubbing tools and an air tank. Kalan lost the ability to breathe.

"Renfield here will help you in your task. Won't you, Renfield?" The robot made no reply.

Trellis, seeing Kalan's terrified look, said, "Oh, don't worry. Renfield won't hurt you. Isn't that right, Renfield?" again, no reply.

Trellis led the still petrified Kalan over to the far end of the room, where the books met the windows. He pressed a small button at the corner of a shelf and it slid behind the other one, revealing a garage. Inside was one of the gliders and an assortment of other equipment. There was a small airlock in the corner for going outside for maintenance or cleaning.

Trellis led Kalan and Renfield to the door of the airlock and motioned for them to go in. She was uneasy about getting into the small room with the robot, but she didn't feel she had a choice at this point. She needed to get through this whole ordeal and get back down the elevator.

Renfield wrapped a harness around Kalan's existing one, which she supposed was useless here with all the light. Then, it attached a rope to the harness and a hoop sticking out of the wall. Kalan watched as the robot did this and thought about how many times she'd come across a fallen scrubber and how some kind of safety line like this would have saved their lives.

Renfield placed a board on the ground and lifted two handles along its sides. Then, it gently nudged her onto the board, her hands naturally grabbed the handles. The board lifted several centimeters off the ground and began floating in place. She tightened her grip apprehensively.

The robot fitted the tank onto one side of the board and a scrub-brush to the other. It motioned for Kalan to put on her mask, so she did, and the robot took a hose from the tank and attached it to a port on the mask. She'd always wanted to know what that was for. A burst of clean air began streaming into the mask. The added pressure burned her lungs even further. She was reaching her limit to how much of this clean, poisonous air she could endure.

The window in front of her opened. She felt a rush of air move out past her and the temperature dropped significantly. The robot gently pushed the board out over the ledge of the building. Then she dropped.

Chapter Ten | The Mission

As the board went into freefall, Kalan instinctively jerked the handles up. The board stopped descending, hovering in the air. She opened her eyes and looked around. She'd fallen into the top layers of the Cloud, but could still see the ledge behind her. The smog swirling around her reminded her of home. She turned her body to look back at the building, the board spun around in response.

I see. The handles control the board. I wish the platforms below were like this.

She experimented with the controls. She found she could make it move in any direction she wanted with the slightest push of the handles. She let it descend slowly into the Cloud until she lost sight of the sky. She took off her mask and breathed in the smog heavily. It was the first completely painless breath she'd taken since getting in the elevator.

I think this is the first full breath I've ever taken; in either life. I never wanted to breathe what was in the air before. I supposed the real Kalan would've felt this way about the air above; we really are different. I'm definitely not the perfect copy the monkey claimed I was.

The memory of what she was took the joy out of flying on the board. She put her mask back on and brought it up out of the Cloud and started looking for the mushrooms.

There they are. Not many of them. I wonder why the robot had trouble. Maybe the mushrooms attacked it to force Trellis to call someone from under the Cloud. I wonder where it ended up. Would anyone even dare go near it?

She flew over to the cluster of mushrooms trailing up from the Cloud. When she tried to get close to the mushrooms, she fumbled with the controls a little. Every time she let go of one of the handles, the board drifted to the side. She found a lock switch and pressed it. The board steadied itself, compensating for wind as it blew in gusts.

She got out the brush and prepared for the task as usual, but as soon as she put the brush against the wall, the first mushroom fell off.

It fell off on its own, I didn't even touch it. Did it even have roots? They usually go deep into the concrete.

She looked down the side of the building and then back at the spot where it was attached.

It's definitely gone. There's no sign of a root structure at all.

She tried another one. It dropped as soon as she got close to it, too.

Could it be all this light? I know it's bothering me a bit. Maybe it's too far away from the Cloud. They eat the acid rain, so maybe they're starving up here. Either way, it's easier for me.

She approached the big bulbous one in the middle of the cluster; all the other ones fell off at the same time. The big one cracked and opened like it was blooming. She backed away, then carefully looked inside. She saw a handgun made of the same harder fungus the bone in her toe was made of. She reached in and took it. The handle fit her hand perfectly like it was sculpted for her.

They probably sculpted it off my dead hand. This must be what the monkey meant. They just needed to get me up here to find this living weapon. Now the rest is up to me, but I still won't do it. They'll have to find some other way. I'm not going to kill for them just because they created me. I won't become their living weapon.

After the gun was removed, the big mushroom fell off too. With nothing left on the building, the job was done. She thought about throwing the gun into the Cloud too, but tucked it into her suit instead.

Just in case. Maybe I'll use it on the monkey when I get back down; show them I do have a choice.

Renfield was waiting for her inside the airlock. She glided into the chamber and stepped off the board. The window behind her closed and the pressure returned to normal. Renfield unhooked the safety line from the harness and attached it to the wall. Through the glass door she saw Trellis approaching.

"Done already? See, I knew you were the one for the task. And you're sure it's completely done? Everything is gone?" Trellis called through the door.

"Yes, everything's gone, roots and all, they shouldn't be able to come back," she replied.

A pleased smile smeared across Trellis' lips. "Wonderful. Very well then, Renfield, kill her and dispose of the body."

"What?" yelled Kalan.

In a panic she grabbed the air tank and hurled it at the robot, knocking it into a release button on the wall. The inside door of the airlock opened and Kalan ran into a startled Trellis. The tank, still attached to Kalan's mask, dragged behind her. She thrashed about to get the mask off, then saw Trellis backing away from her against the window and Renfield getting to its feet. Trellis was between her and the door to the apartment.

What do I do now? Do I run? Could I make it to the elevator before the robot tears me apart? she thought.

"Kill her, I say! Kill her!" screamed Trellis, pointing at Kalan. She reached into her suit, pulled out the gun, and pointed it at Trellis. The Marquese's eyes widened with shock.

"Woah! Okay, hold on," Trellis begged. The robot moved toward Kalan but Trellis lifted his hand when he saw her tighten her grip on the strange looking gun.

He shouted, "Renfield, stop!" The robot complied. He looked at Kalan and began to regain his composure.

"Kalan, was it? What are you doing? You don't want to hurt me," he said in a patronizing tone.

"That's funny, a moment ago you were the one ordering your robot to kill me," Kalan replied.

"Okay, I admit, that was foolish of me. Come, we can work this out. Let's go back in the other room and we'll talk," he moved to leave the garage but Kalan moved around him so she was the same distance to the door as he was and pointed the gun more menacingly at him.

"Don't move!" she shouted. "Tell me why you wanted to kill me. I did what you wanted, why not just let me go home? And what was all that talk about being a spokesperson for your group if you were just going to kill me? Talk."

"All right, I'll be honest with you. There is no group. No one wants to help you lowers, and we already know everything about you," there was derision in his voice now. "Everyone knows about how you live down there in your disgusting Cloud pit. We grow up learning all about it; the violence, the poverty, the perpetual darkness. And we monitor you all, most of the city is auto-surveyed constantly. How do you think we're able to send robots down to get any guns that show up down there by mistake?

"Speaking of which, I've never seen anything quite like this piece you've got pointed at me. Care to tell me where you got it?" he paused, but Kalan gave no answer.

"I thought not. I should have known not to bring one of you up here. They all said it was a bad idea, but I didn't want to lose another Renfield to those stupid mushrooms. They're expensive, you

131

know. You aren't. You're worthless. There are millions of you running around down there, all the same, all mindless, violent slaves with no potential for true humanity. You're good for one thing, making us rich, and with any luck, me even richer.

"I AM trying to rid the city of all the fungus, I wasn't lying about that; but not out of some noble, profitless sentiment. I'm doing it because my business is the chemical spray that keeps the buildings from eroding in the acid rains. The mushrooms eat the acid, so they make my business obsolete in the mushroom district. I've even heard rumors that some of the building owners are getting restless with my price hikes. They've been trying to cultivate the mushrooms so they don't have to pay me. Well, that's not gonna glide! I'm going to destroy their precious loophole, and then I'll be able to charge them whatever I want and they'll have to pay it. Or they could just sell their buildings to me.

"I don't expect you to understand what I'm talking about. You don't even have money. We don't even pay you, we give you false hopes with little bits of electricity. Look around you, we get all that electricity for free from the sun. We just use it to control you; make sure you're all too weak to fight. That is, if you ever even found out about us.

"That's the best part, you don't even know you're slaves. You don't even know life could be anything more than that dystopian nightmare down there. But here's the thing; every dystopia is someone's utopia. And yours is mine.

"I don't know who you're working for, and I don't care. You can't do anything to me. Even if that weird thing you've got works, which I doubt, I'm mostly prosthetic, remember? Whatever part of me you hit will just be a call away from being replaced and you'll be dead."

Kalan saw the robot moving out of the corner of her eye.

Distraction. That's his plan.

She moved away from the robot, trying to keep an eye on both while keeping the gun pointed at Trellis. Kalan had had enough of this.

She shouted, "Stop! I didn't want to do this, they made me. And then I still wasn't going to do it because I don't want to hurt anyone. None of this has anything to do with me. Not the real me.

"I was just going to do your task and go back, even though I don't think I have anything to go back to. Then you had to go and be a monstrous piece of shit! Even after you tried to kill me, I still would have walked away, I don't want any of this! But now I can't. Not after you showed me what you really are, what you're trying to do, what you ARE doing to everyone down there. Why would you do this? I don't understand. What did we ever do to you?

"You say we're the violent ones, but the only violence I've ever seen down there are people trying to survive. Sometimes they go too far, but that's because they don't know when their next meal is going to be or where they're going to sleep next. They get desperate, and it's for no reason. You could make sure we don't ever have to starve, but you just want more for yourself? That's true violence!

"You say we don't have any potential?! It's because you took it away from us. My sister will never have ambitions beyond finding things in a pile of YOUR trash because you stole away our choice about how to live our lives.

"I can't let you live now! Not after knowing that. And I have to tell them, I have to let them know about you and all the rest of your kind up here; about how we're just your slaves and we don't even know it. Just like you said.

"So, that's what I'm going to do. I'm going to kill you, and I'm going to go back and let everyone know; and then we'll come for all of you."

"And how do you plan to do that, huh? Weren't you listening? You can't kill me with that thing; and Renfield will rip you apart the moment you try. You'll never get out of here alive, and your people will never know anything. Your sister will just think you died in an alley somewhere, like the rest of you filth. Until she dies the same way."

Kalan hesitated. She didn't know what to do.

She tried to think, *He's right, I probably can't kill him, I'm not even sure if this thing will work, and that robot will grab me as soon as I fire. Why did this happen to me? I never hurt anyone. No. It doesn't matter, I'm here and I have a mission. As much as I hate to admit it, that monkey-thing was right about this guy. He has to die. But I have to get back down, too. Otherwise, it'll all be for nothing. They'll continue working us to dust for their own profit. I have to get out of here; I have to get back to Sett. No matter how.*

The next moment, four things happened in quick succession. Kalan formed a plan in her mind; the cleaning ball robots rolled in the door, which Kalan glanced at; Renfield saw her momentary lapse in attention and lunged at her; and then Kalan acted on her plan.

She fired the gun and ran as fast as she could toward Trellis. The entire gun exploded in her hand when she pulled the trigger. A cloud of spores filled the room and a small hard projectile launched from the front of the gun, propelled by the explosion; but instead of hitting Trellis, it went straight through the window behind him. Then, Kalan tackled him into the weakened window and they both fell with the shattered glass.

Trellis attempted to fight as they fell, his prosthetic limbs trying to tear Kalan's fungus body apart. They fell into the Cloud. It felt like millions of tiny needles pelting them at once. Their bodies twisted and spun around each other as the light disappeared and all was the blackness of the toxic Cloud.

Trellis screamed from the pain of the ice particles polishing the flesh from the parts of his body that weren't artificial; he struggled to breathe in the toxin filled air. He was gasping desperately. At the same time, Kalan was having a strange reaction to the Cloud; her cells were drinking in the noxious minerals, and the ice crystals bounced off her tougher, less elastic, skin facsimile. Her body expanded as the fungus absorbed the nourishing toxins. Her skin split and burst open as she expanded; the pain was all-encompassing.

For two and a half minutes they fell, twisting and turning their way to their inevitable deaths; eventually coming through the bottom of the Cloud into the hazy neon city below. But still they fell. Kalan saw the salvage yards. She twisted herself so they would land with Trellis on top.

If I can keep him on top, maybe he'll be intact enough to let them see there are people above. Maybe they'll understand. It's all I can do now.

They hit the concrete ground at 53 meters per second [122 mph].

The sound was like a crack of thunder. The street cratered under them. A crowd formed to see what happened. Kalan was barely still conscious; a fading light moving away from her in a fog. Her face was cracked open like a smashed pumpkin, but through the darkness, she saw her.

Sett was there, at the edge of the crater. Kalan couldn't hear anymore, but she saw the recognition in her eyes. Sett spotted her suit and '0' pip. She rushed down to Kalan's side, crying and screaming. Kalan fought the darkness as long as she could, and with her last moment of consciousness, she said, "You are slaves. Find them. Fight them."

End

About the Author

T S Galindo grew up on the East Coast of the United States. He has a B.S. in Mechanical Engineering and works as a Mechanical Designer while pondering the absurdity of existence. He suffers from curiosity, creativity, anxiety, and depression. He lives with his wife, Sam, and their two cats, DeLorean and Taco.

Printed in Great Britain
by Amazon